The Case of the Hurricane Hounds

A Thousand Islands Doggy Inn Mystery

B.R. Snow

Copyright © 2017 B.R. Snow
ISBN: 978-1-942691-26-6

Website: www.brsnow.net/
Twitter: @BernSnow
Facebook: facebook.com/bernsnow

Cover Design: Reggie Cullen
Cover Photo: James R. Miller

Other Books by B.R. Snow

The Thousand Islands Doggy Inn Mysteries

- The Case of the Abandoned Aussie
- The Case of the Brokenhearted Bulldog
- The Case of the Caged Cockers
- The Case of the Dapper Dandie Dinmont
- The Case of the Eccentric Elkhound
- The Case of the Faithful Frenchie
- The Case of the Graceful Goldens

The Whiskey Run Chronicles

- Episode 1 – The Dry Season Approaches
- Episode 2 – Friends and Enemies
- Episode 3 – Let the Games Begin
- Episode 4 – Enter the Revenuer
- Episode 5 – A Changing Landscape
- Episode 6 – Entrepreneurial Spirits
- Episode 7 – All Hands On Deck
- The Whiskey Run Chronicles – The Complete Volume 1

The Damaged Posse

- American Midnight
- Larrikin Gene
- Sneaker World
- Summerman
- The Duplicates

Other Books

- Divorce Hotel
- Either Ore

To Dog Lovers Everywhere

Chapter 1

The plane shuddered as it passed through a small patch of turbulence, and I pressed my back hard against the seat, closed my eyes, and dug my nails into the armrests on either side of me. Both Josie and Chef Claire woke with a start and glared at me then examined the matching sets of indentations on their forearms.

"Uh. Ow," Chef Claire said, rubbing her forearm.

"Yeah, thanks for that," Josie said, yawning. "I was right in the middle of a great dream. I was being chased down a white-sand beach by this gorgeous guy, and I was just about to let him catch me."

"You want to switch dreams?" Chef Claire said. "Mine was of me cooking at the restaurant, and no matter how fast I was filling the orders, they just kept stacking up. What do you think it means?"

"That you probably need a vacation," Josie said, folding her hands in her lap as she gave me another dirty look.

"Makes sense," Chef Claire said, nodding as she stared out the window at the ocean seven miles straight down.

"How can you two sleep when we're about to drop out of the sky like a rock?" I said, staring straight ahead at the back of the seat in front of me.

1

"Well, I'm starting a week's vacation and don't plan on getting a lot of rest. And I need my beauty sleep," Josie said.

"Yeah, you need beauty sleep like our dogs need another chew toy," I said.

"Aren't you sweet," Josie said, closing her eyes. "Besides, I want to be well rested when we crash into the ocean."

"You're not funny," I said.

"Disagree."

A flight attendant arrived with our drink orders, and we all lowered our seat trays. The attendant handed us our glasses and bags of peanuts that weren't big enough to get a zoo animal's attention. We stared down at the peanuts and Josie shook her head sadly and looked up at the attendant.

"Pitiful," Josie said.

"Yes, I know," the attendant said, obviously very familiar with the complaint. "Would you like another bag?"

"No, thanks, that's okay," Josie said, reaching for the large carry on she had stuffed under the seat in front of her. "I think I've got it covered."

Josie removed three Tupperware containers and placed them on her tray. She removed the plastic lids, and the attendant stared down at what was inside. Josie anticipated the question and pointed at each item as she outlined what was on the menu.

"Bacon wrapped barbecue shrimp. Fried jalapeno poppers with bacon and cream cheese. And bacon walnut brownies."

"I'm sensing a theme here," the attendant said.

"Yeah, I'm on a bit of a bacon kick lately," Josie said. "Help yourself. Chef Claire made enough to feed a small army."

"Actually," Chef Claire said, reaching over for one of the brownies. "A small army would be easier to feed than this one. Try one of the shrimp."

"I really shouldn't," the attendant said, looking in both directions before selecting and taking a bite of one of the shrimp. "Oh, my goodness. That's so good. It's a…what's the word I'm looking for?"

"Knee-buckler," I whispered as I continued to stare straight ahead gripping the armrests as the plane roared through another patch of turbulence.

"That's it," the attendant said, helping herself to one of the bacon and cream cheese poppers. "These are incredible."

"How can you people eat at a time like this?" I said, tightening my death grip on the armrests and closing my eyes.

"Hey, if you're going to be clinging to a flotation device in shark infested waters, you don't want to do it on an empty stomach," Chef Claire said.

Josie and the attendant chortled. I ignored their laughter, but Chef Claire's comment resonated. I opened my eyes and glanced at the Tupperware.

"Maybe you've got a point there," I said, reaching for three of the shrimp, a popper, and two brownies.

"Is there anything else you need?" the attendant said, accepting the brownie Josie was holding out.

"Just an empty seat on my right."

"Still not funny."

"Disagree."

"I'll see what I can do," the attendant said, laughing as she rolled her cart up the aisle.

"How much longer do we have?" I said, closing my eyes as I chewed a mouthful of brownie.

"I guess that depends," Josie said.

"On what?"

"On whether or not we die immediately on impact."

"Josie, please," I said, opening my eyes to glare at her.

"A plane crash is the least of our worries," Josie said.

"Is it now?"

"Yes. Didn't you say that your mother is picking us up at the airport?"

"Don't remind me," I said.

My mother's reputation for being a lead-foot driver devoid of patience was well deserved. I could only imagine how her usual method for getting from point A to B using whatever speed or route that struck her fancy would work on what I assumed would be a road system vastly different from the one we were used to.

"They drive on the left down here," Chef Claire said, reaching for another brownie.

"Like that's going to make any difference to my mother."

The plane shook again for several seconds, and my stomach churned and threatened to return a whole lot of bacon. I fumbled in the seat pocket in front of me, found the bag I was looking for, and focused on my breathing as sweat began to form on my forehead.

"Can you make it to the bathroom without throwing up on me on your way out?" Josie said, quickly putting the lids back on the Tupperware.

"I don't like my chances."

"Then just sit there very still."

I did just that, managed to keep everything down, and thirty minutes later the plane landed without incident then slowly taxied and came to a stop. We grabbed our carry on luggage and headed down the stairs to the tarmac, then were buffeted by a strong warm breeze that seemed appropriate for the eighty-degree temperature. I felt a bit better as soon as my feet were on solid ground, and I made the short walk across the tarmac and stepped inside the air-conditioned terminal.

I saw my mother before she knew we'd made it off the plane. She was sporting a tan that was so perfect I immediately assumed it came from a spray gun. She was wearing white shorts and a colorful floral-patterned blouse along with sandals and a pair of sunglasses I knew cost a small fortune. I knew this because I was left speechless and wondering if she'd lost her mind when she showed me the price tag while we were shopping in Montreal at Les Étoffes.

She was chatting and laughing with a handful of people and seemed totally relaxed. When she saw us coming through immigration, she excused herself from the others and waited with a huge smile.

"Hello, darling," she said, crushing me with a hug and a kiss.

"Hi, Mom," I said, grabbing her shoulders to look at her then going back in for a second hug. "You look great."

"I wish I could say the same for you, darling," she said, frowning. "Bad flight?"

"The worst," I said, draping my carry on bag over my shoulder.

"The plane took off and landed safely, right?" she said, cocking her head at me.

"Yeah."

"Did you throw up?"

"No."

"Then you had a good flight," she said, patting my hand. "Count your blessings. Hello, girls. Welcome to Grand Cayman."

"Hey, Mrs. C.," Josie said.

"Thanks for picking us up," Chef Claire said.

They exchanged hugs and kisses, and my mom gestured for us to follow her to the baggage area. We grabbed our luggage and followed her outside to the parking area. She had a bounce in her step, and I was again amazed by her energy. Two identical four-wheel drive jeeps with the tops removed sat next to each other.

"Ladies, this is Henry," my mother said, draping her arm around the shoulder of the man who was beaming at us. "Henry, this is my daughter Suzy, and her friends and business partners, Josie and Chef Claire."

"It's so nice to finally meet all of you," Henry said. "Mrs. C. has told me so much about all of you." Then he forced himself to stop staring at Josie and looked at Chef Claire. "Do you really prefer to be called Chef Claire instead of just Claire?"

"I do," she said, nodding. "Weird, huh?"

"I've been called much worse," he said, shrugging.

"Henry, would you mind loading all the luggage and taking it back to the house?" my mother said, reaching into her pocket for her car keys.

"Not at all," he said. "I'll see you there later."

He gently arranged all our luggage into the back of the jeep, waved, and drove off. My mother gestured at the jeep she was driving, and Josie and Chef Claire climbed into the back seat. I sat down in the passenger seat next to my mother.

"He seems nice," I said.

"Henry's wonderful," my mother said, slowly backing the jeep out. "He keeps an eye on the place for me when I'm not around. But when I'm down here, he moves out of the main house into the guest cottage."

"What does he do for you?" I said, trying to remember what she had told me over the years.

"Pretty much everything," she said, putting the jeep in forward and inching toward the exit. "And by the way, he handles the lawn and garden, so you'll see him around outside. As such, when you're sunbathing by the pool, you might want to keep your top on. That is unless you're feeling adventurous, darling."

"I've been here ten minutes, Mom," I said, staring out at the road. "Don't start."

"Whatever you say," she said, grinning as she glanced through the rear-view mirror into the backseat. "You ladies feel like stopping on the way home for some lunch?"

Josie glanced at Chef Claire who thought about it then nodded. Josie caught my mother's eye in the mirror and raised both thumbs.

"I could eat."

Chapter 2

The scenery changed soon after we left the area around the airport, a section of developed land my mother called sand-based industrial. Whatever the heck that meant. We headed into the center of George Town, the capital of the Cayman Islands with a population around 30,000. As we drove along the main street, I glanced around at the shops and preponderance of tourists wandering the street. I must have been frowning because my mother slowed down and glanced back and forth between me and the road for several seconds.

"Yes, darling?"

"This seems oddly familiar," I said. "You didn't bring me here when I was a kid, did you?"

"No. But it'll come to you," she said, smiling as she turned onto West Bay Road. "Up there on the left is the famous 7 Mile Beach. My place is just up the road at the far end."

I glanced over at the magnificent stretch of sand and ocean and nodded absentmindedly as I continued to deal with the déjà vu I was experiencing. Finally, it dawned on me why the place looked familiar.

"It's a Carribean version of Clay Bay, only bigger," I blurted. "That's why it seems so familiar, right?"

"Very good, darling," she said, waving to someone on the street. "They have a very similar vibe. Of course, the tourist season here is a bit more year-round if you catch my drift."

"Yeah, I got it, Mrs. C.," Josie said from the backseat. "And right now at home, the drifts are about six-feet high. And they're not made of sand."

"Then aren't you glad you're here?" my mother said, laughing as she waved to a man standing on the side of the street waiting to cross. "Oh, there's Gerald."

"Who's Gerald?" I said, studying the man who obviously wasn't a tourist.

"Oh, he's the Finance Minister," my mother said, slowing down to avoid running over a small group of tourists.

"Well, he must be a very busy man," I said.

"Why's that, darling?"

"Because it looks like there's a bank every ten feet. How many are there?"

"Too many to count, I'm sure," my mother said, not taking her eyes off the road.

"Should I even ask why a place this small would need anywhere near that number of banks?"

"Probably not, darling," my said, glancing over at me with a smile. "But you'll meet Gerald tonight at dinner."

"Okay, maybe I'll just ask him," I said, glancing into the backseat. "The Finance Minister is coming for dinner tonight."

Way beyond being surprised by anyone my mother was on a first-name basis with, they both shrugged at the news and continued to glance out at the ocean.

"That's a lot of cruise ships," Chef Claire said.

"Yes, this is a busy time of year for them," my mother said. "The port can't handle their size, so they anchor offshore, and the passengers are ferried to shore."

"I count seven of them," Chef Claire said.

"I think it's cruise ship mating season," Josie deadpanned. "They head for warmer waters when they're ready to make babies."

"What does a cruise ship baby look like?" Chef Claire said, laughing.

"I think they start out as runabouts. Or maybe tour boats," Josie said, frowning.

"They head for warmer water?" I said.

"Yeah."

"Like the whales?" I said, giving her a blank stare.

"Exactly," she said, grinning at me. "Still not funny?"

"Still not funny."

"Did you forget to pack your sense of humor, darling?" my mother said, putting on her turn signal and checking all her mirrors. "I thought it was very funny, Josie."

"Thanks, Mrs. C."

My mother pulled off the road and parked in front of a beachside restaurant she couldn't stop raving about. She led the way in, stopped to chat with several people, and five minutes later I had a long list of names and faces to remember. We sat down at a patio table near the sand, and my mother took the liberty of ordering Mudslides for all of us, a popular local drink made of equal parts vodka, Kahlua, and Bailey's Irish Cream over crushed ice. I took a sip, then another and nodded.

"Apart from the ice, there's nothing non-alcoholic in this thing," I said.

"There's a cherry on top," Chef Claire said. "And I'm picking up a touch of cinnamon."

"Well, that changes everything then," I said, grinning through another sip. "Now I don't feel so bad. But don't let me have more than six of these."

While everyone else stuffed themselves on fish tacos, I stuck to my guns regarding my aversion to all things fish and had a burger and fries. Everything was delicious, and now full and recovered from the flight, we climbed back into the jeep. I watched my mother slowly make her way back onto the road that would take us to her house. Eventually, I couldn't help but ask the question.

"Are you sick, Mom?" I said, glancing over at her.

"Sick? Absolutely not. I feel wonderful. Why do you ask?"

"Because you're driving like a normal person."

"This is the way I always drive down here, darling. Are you in a hurry to get somewhere?"

"Me?" I said, exasperated. "I'm talking about you, Mom. You always drive like a maniac."

"Ah," she said, waving the comment away. "The island is only about thirty miles long. Why on earth would I need to hurry?"

A few minutes later, she turned into a driveway and wound her way through a dazzling collection of native plants and flowers. Then she parked in the circular drive in front of the house next to the other jeep Henry had been driving. While I had seen photos of the house several times, they hadn't come close to capturing just how beautiful the place was. It was a sprawling bright white single-story structure of stone and stucco, and the smell of the ocean was impossible to miss. As if reading my mind, my mother smiled at me.

"The ocean's right on the other side of the house," she said. "And the pool is over there to your right."

"Geez, Mom," I said, putting my hands on my hips as I glanced around the property. "It's incredible."

"Thank you, darling. And someday it will be all yours," she said, squeezing my arm affectionately.

"Mom, I don't want your house."

"I'll take it," Josie said, laughing as she looked around. "You outdid yourself, Mrs. C."

"I've been telling you two for years how beautiful it is down here," she said, heading for the front door. "Now, why don't you get changed and go for a swim and get a bit of sun? All three of you look like ghosts."

"Mom, it was zero when we left this morning. It's not exactly tanning weather."

"Yes, I saw the weather report," she said, grinning. "Now do you understand why I'm here?"

"Yeah, I get it," I said, continuing to take the house and property in.

"I wonder if they need another good restaurant in town," Chef Claire said.

"Don't get any ideas," Josie said, gently punching her on the arm.

"It's something to think about," Chef Claire said. "And I'm sure they have lots of dogs here that need help."

"Geez, Chef Claire," Josie said, shaking her head.

"I'm sorry. I forgot."

My mood turned dark as I pondered how much I already missed Chloe and the rest of the dogs at the Inn.

"Oh, I hope they're all doing okay," I said.

"Suzy, they're fine," Josie said, still glaring at Chef Claire for broaching the subject.

"Don't you miss Captain?"

"Of course I miss him," she said. "But all the dogs are in very good hands. And we're only going to be gone for a week."

"Maybe I should give Sammy and Jill a quick call just to make sure," I said, reaching for my phone.

"Why don't you wait long enough for them to realize that you're actually not there?" Josie said, grabbing my phone and tossing it to Chef Claire.

"Give that back," I said.

"Maybe later," Chef Claire said, tossing my phone into her bag.

"Come on, let's get changed and go for a swim," Josie said as she looked up at the sky. "That's odd. The weather report said to expect sunny and warm all week. If I didn't know better, I'd swear there was a storm moving in."

Chapter 3

We changed, went for a swim in the pool, then stretched out in lounge chairs and napped for an hour. I woke already feeling a touch of sunburn. I pressed a finger against my shoulder and watched my skin color go from red to pale then back to red.

"Okay," I said, sitting up and draping a towel over my shoulders. "I'm almost medium rare."

"Me too," Josie said. "That sun's intense."

"Yeah, I'm done for the day," Chef Claire said. "Besides, the clouds are starting to move in."

"Let's go for a walk on the beach," Josie said, standing up and pulling on a large men's dress shirt she left unbuttoned.

"Sounds good," I said, pulling on shorts and a tee shirt.

"I think I'm going to head inside for a shower and a nap before dinner," Chef Claire said. "Have fun."

We watched her head for the house then walked down a sandy path that led directly to the beach. We stepped onto the magnificent stretch of white sand and looked around in both directions.

"Left will take us to big resorts and tourists," Josie said. "Right looks a lot quieter."

I knew the direction we both wanted, and I headed right and made my way down to the water's edge. We walked in the ankle-high water, but the waves reaching shore appeared to be getting a bit bigger as we continued up the quiet stretch of beach.

"The weather seems a bit strange, doesn't it?" Josie said, frowning.

"Yeah, I think you're right about a storm heading our way," I said, glancing up at the sky. "Just our luck, huh?"

"It's okay. I'll take eighty and rainy," she said, then stopped walking and placed a hand on my forearm.

"What is it?" I said, panicking as I searched the immediate stretch of water. "Shark?"

"No, you idiot," she said, laughing. "Over there in that stretch of palms. Is that a bloodhound?"

"Yeah, I think you're right," I said, squinting.

The bloodhound was lumbering back and forth on the edge of the palms and seemed to be on the lookout for intruders. We slowly made our way toward him, but when he saw us he gave us a half-howl, half-growl and we hung back. The palms were located at a spot where a grass lawn met the sand in front of a large house that appeared to be vacant.

"Is there something wrong with him?" I said, squinting into the diffused glare of the sun.

"He's agitated," Josie said. "Other than that he seems fine. But it doesn't look like he wants us around."

"He's probably a stray," I said. "When we get back to the house, let's check to see if there's an animal shelter nearby. Maybe they can come and check it out."

"Good call," Josie said.

A gust of wind hammered both of us, and we staggered back a few steps in the soft sand. The bloodhound disappeared back into the palms.

"Let's head back to the house," I said. "My mom said we were eating early. But with this wind, I'm not sure we'll be able to barbecue outside."

"Oh, no," Josie deadpanned as we turned around and headed in the other direction. "Forced to eat inside that gorgeous house. Not the briar patch."

"It is nice," I said, nodding.

"Nice? Suzy, that place would have to get blown away by a hurricane before it would even come close to being called nice. It's magnificent."

"Let's hope it doesn't come to that," I said, raising my hands to block the sand that was swirling around my face.

"Man, something is definitely headed our way," she said, locking arms with me as we trudged through the sand. "Can I ask you something?"

"Sure. Just speak up so I can hear you," I said, lowering my head as another gust of wind swirled around us.

"Do you ever talk to your mom about how she and your dad made all their money?"

"Only in general terms," I said. "Real estate and the stock market is about as much detail as she'll go into. Why do you ask?"

"Oh, you know me. I'm just being a bit of a snoop."

"I thought that was my job."

"Well, I figured, what with you being on vacation and all..."

Chapter 4

The guests my mother had invited to dinner were, per her normal pattern, a diverse collection of people that included some corporate types and their spouses, an ex-pat couple who'd escaped the cold weather, a successful local artist who sold landscape paintings by the dozens to cruise ship tourists, and Gerald, the Finance Minister we'd seen earlier on the street.

My mother, nonplussed at first by the sudden change of weather, had huddled with Henry and decided to move the grill onto the verandah to avoid as much of the wind as possible. Chef Claire had offered her help and was immediately rebuffed by my mother who said that she was forbidden to go anywhere near the kitchen for any reason other than to grab a fresh drink for the duration of her stay. But Henry seemed to know his way around a grill, and soon the smell of fresh local lobster and assorted meats drifted across the verandah.

I sipped my second Mudslide, not counting the one I'd had at lunch, and tried to focus on the *creative applications of arbitrage in underdeveloped economies* a financial consultant was breathlessly explaining to me as he kept sneaking glances at my legs and patting my hand every time I drifted off to worry about the bloodhound we'd seen on the beach. Ten minutes into the conversation, I was already planning my escape but was trapped.

And I returned the sly smile my mother was giving me from the other side of the verandah with a narrow-eyed glare.

Josie and Chef Claire were laughing as they chatted with the local artist named Sky, and I nodded at Josie to switch chairs and change conversations with me. She smiled at my obvious discomfort and shook her head that let me know in no uncertain terms that I was on my own. I made a face at her then refocused on the consultant and caught the tail end of why guaranteed points and an interest rate at least one percent below prime were essential elements in any commercial deal these days that involved a real estate component.

"Fascinating," I said, getting up out of my chair. "Excuse me, I need to use the ladies room."

"I'll be right here waiting," the consultant whose name I'd already successfully forgotten said.

"Don't worry, I won't forget," I said, making a beeline for the door that led inside to the living room.

Gerald, the Finance Minister, was sitting on a couch and finishing a phone call. He slipped his phone into his shirt pocket and beamed at me and patted the couch for me to sit down next to him.

"I see you managed to escape Timothy," he said, grinning at me.

"Yes, well, I've never been much for financial conversations. I'd rather watch paint dry," I said, then felt the need to apologize. "No offense."

"None taken," he said, chuckling. "They're not my favorite either. But don't tell my boss."

"I won't," I said, immediately warming up to him. "Am I picking up a trace of a British accent?"

"Just a bit. I spent several years in London while I was getting my education. I picked the accent up, and some of it stuck."

"How do you know my mother?"

"It's a small island, and your mother has a big personality," he said with a grin that seemed permanently etched on. "But I've known her for years."

"Did you know my father?"

"Yes, I did," he said, his smile fading a bit as he looked out at the ocean. "He was a good man. I miss having him around."

"Did you work together?"

"We did some deals together, yes. After he died your mother picked things up without missing a beat."

"You still work with her?" I said, cocking my head at him as my snoop alarm went off.

"Of course," he said, shrugging. "Your mother is a genius."

"Not a word I would use in her presence," I said, laughing. "What sort of things are you two up to?"

"I thought you didn't enjoy financial conversations."

"You're right, I don't," I said, making a mental note to have a little chat with my mother. "What's up with this weather?"

"I'm sure it's just a thunderstorm. It should pass by morning," he said.

We glanced up when we saw everyone heading inside and making their way to the dining room table that was set for fourteen.

"It appears dinner is served," Gerald said, standing up.

"Would you mind if I sat next to you at dinner?" I said, glancing at Timothy who was hovering near the dining room table and glancing in my direction.

"I'd be honored," he said, bowing slightly. "As long as we can get to those two seats between your mother and your friend Josie, I think we'll be fine."

"So, you don't want to sit next to him either?" I said.

"Eat dinner next to Timothy?" he said, grinning at me. "I'd rather watch paint dry."

I followed him to the table, waited for him to sit down next to my mother, then sat down between him and Josie who was still engaged in an animated conversation with the artist.

"Thanks for the help," I said, nudging her with an elbow.

"I didn't want to interrupt," she said. "It looked like you were having so much fun."

"I owe you one," I said, keeping a close eye on a tray of steaks that was being passed around.

As I started to build my dinner plate, I glanced around the table at my mother's guests. I'd been introduced to everyone except the two couples sitting across from me who had arrived late at the same time.

"Who are the folks across the table from us?" I whispered, leaning close to Gerald.

"The couple on the left is Alex and Prunella Smith," he whispered back. "But he goes by the nickname Wily."

"Wily as in clever in business?" I said, sneaking a peek at him.

"No, although he's done very well," Gerald said, selecting a lobster tail from the tray in front of him. "Wily as in trying to sleep with every woman he can and not get caught."

"I see," I said. "And I suppose that's why his wife looks like she's working as his bodyguard?"

Gerald chuckled and nodded. "Yes, over the years, Prunella has been forced to adopt the mentality of a…oh, what's the term I'm looking for?"

"Guard dog?" I whispered.

"Exactly," he said, sliding a piece of lobster into his mouth.

"So, I take it Wily has, sticking with the dog terms for the moment, a hard time staying on the porch?"

"Yes," Gerald said, laughing loud enough to get my mother's attention. "The nickname is hard-earned. And Wily is obviously quite taken with your friend Josie."

"Now, there's a surprise," I said, shaking my head. "What about the couple sitting next to them?"

"Thomas and Sally Witherspoon," Gerald said. "He runs one of the big banks down here. She spends her time doing charity work and trying to keep up with Wily."

"Really? The two of them are together?"

"Oh, no," Gerald said, selecting a grilled skewer of cherry tomatoes and mushrooms. "I was referring to their scorecards. You know, the running totals of their indiscretions She also has, as you say, a hard time staying on the porch."

"I see. So, Wily and Sally have never…you know."

"Oh, I'd be very surprised if they hadn't," Gerald said. "They're both like the tourists who go out of their way to visit as many countries as they can while they're on vacation regardless of how little time they get to spend there. As long as they get their passport stamped, they're happy."

"Just so they can say they've been there," I said, nodding.

"Yes."

"Sad," I said, glancing at Prunella who was giving Josie a dirty look. "So, everybody here works in finance?"

"Pretty much," Gerald said, glancing around the table. "Except for Sky, of course."

"Good name for a landscape artist," I said, taking a bite of steak.

As I ate, I glanced around the table at the others and wondered what it was about them that had caught my mother's attention. But as I listened to the conversations and heard the genuine laughter, I decided that my mother's only criteria for inclusion seemed to be having an interest in other people combined with an ability to hold up their end of a conversation.

And maybe money.

It was pretty clear that everybody around the table, with the possible exception of Henry, was loaded.

Then I discarded that notion because I had years of experience with my mother at home in Clay Bay and the question of how much money someone had never seemed to be a factor regarding who she spent her time with.

But this was the Cayman Islands, the offshore home to billions of dollars.

Maybe her circle of friends was different down here for different reasons.

Maybe this group of people just happened to keep her mind sharp, and her sense of humor at the ready.

Maybe I was just trying to read too much into it.

I forced myself to relax and transition into full vacation mode, but something nagged at me. My mother glanced over at me and noticed the frown on my face. Then she caught my eye and gave me a look I recognized immediately. She didn't use it on me often, but when she did the message behind it was abundantly clear and straight to the point.

Let it go.

Chapter 5

After dinner, I was sitting next to the ex-pat couple on the couch. They were originally from Buffalo and had moved here almost ten years ago after a particularly nasty winter storm when the husband, Bill, had slipped on the ice and gotten a concussion and three cracked ribs. As soon as he was released from the hospital, his wife Jerry explained they had jumped on a plane and not looked back. And as soon as they learned that it was my first trip to the Caymans, they became my self-appointed tour guides.

Jerry, a good looking woman with big hair and a big voice, jumped in first.

"Well, obviously, you don't need to worry about finding a beach to hang out on," she said, good-naturedly. "Your mother has certainly taken care of that."

"Magnificent house," Bill said, nodding. "And 7 Mile Beach is our favorite. It's one of those spots that makes you genuflect to Mother Nature. We like to sit in our lounge chairs in shallow water and sip cocktails. You can't get much more relaxed than that."

"It sounds great," I said, my head starting to swivel as they took turns speaking.

"Absolutely," Jerry said. "And make sure you take some time to explore George Town. A lot of people forget to do that. It only takes a couple of hours. There's lots of great stores and boutiques. And the local architecture is very interesting."

"Yes, of course. George Town is a great way to kill a couple of hours," Bill said, fighting for airtime. "But it's all manmade and way overdeveloped. She'll want to spend most of her time in the water. Do you snorkel?" he said, then continued without waiting for my response. "The water down here is incredibly clear and-"

"Oh, snorkeling," Jerry said. "Of course. And you definitely need to visit Stingray City."

"Stingray City? Is that an underwater bar?" I said, trying to remember the term from the tourist brochures my mother had given us that I'd only glanced at.

Bill and Jerry laughed and took sips of their Mudslides in perfect rhythm with each other.

"Stingray City is a spot near here where you can pet and feed the stingrays," Bill said.

"The fishermen used to clean their catch and toss the remains into the water. Over the years, the stingrays have gotten used to people," Jerry said. "And you can snorkel around them, or just stand in the water. They'll actually swim right up to you and nuzzle you looking for a treat."

"Gee, I don't know. Except for dogs, I'm not much of a nuzzler," I said, frowning. "Especially with creatures that can kill me."

"Oh, you'll be fine," Bill said. "Just don't try to pull their tail."

"Okay, no tail pulling. Got it."

"And no trip to the Caymans is complete without a visit to Turtle Farm," Jerry said, glancing at her husband whose head became a bobblehead doll for a moment as he nodded his agreement.

"Absolutely," Bill said. "They raise and protect the turtles then release them back into the ocean."

"And they make the best turtle soup," Jerry said.

"Yes, it's fantastic," Bill said.

"So, I take it their protection is a bit spotty at times?" I said.

"What?" Jerry said, glancing at her husband. "Oh, I get it. That's funny. You must get your sense of humor from your mom."

"Yes, indeed. Most amusing," Bill said. "Just like her mother."

"You really think my mother is funny?" I said, doing my best not to frown.

"Of course," Jerry said. "Don't you?"

"Yeah, I guess," I said, nodding. "But probably not for the same reasons as you."

They glanced at each other and shrugged simultaneously. Then Bill's expression turned serious, and he stared at me.

"But if swimming, snorkeling, fishing, stingrays, and turtles don't interest you, I only have one thing to say to you."

"What's that?" I said, taken aback by his sudden mood swing.

"Then you can just go to Hell," he whispered.

"I beg your pardon?"

Bill maintained his pose, then he and his wife roared with laughter.

"You're awful," she said, playfully punching him on the shoulder.

"I'm sorry, Suzy," he said. "But I couldn't resist. Hell is actually a very small town just north of here. A lot of people go there to see the volcanic rock and grab a souvenir tee shirt."

"You can send postcards to all your friends from the post office," Jerry said. "And when it comes in the mail, it'll have a postmark from Hell. Get it?"

"I got it," I said, smiling. "But if I can't find the time to visit, I can always just mail them from here."

"What?" Bill said, then burst into laughter again. "Good one. You are too funny."

"Just like her mother," Jerry said.

My mother approached and stood in the middle of the living room and called for everyone's attention.

"I'm sorry to interrupt," she said, holding her hands in front of her as she glanced around. "And I'm about to break my cardinal rule about having the television on during a party. But I think it would be a good idea for us to take a look at the weather report. The wind is continuing to pick up, and it's started to rain quite hard."

Everyone murmured their assent, and my mother grabbed the remote and turned the TV on. A serious weatherman was talking and pointing at a large yellow and red object on the map of the Caribbean behind him.

"Again, I want to emphasize that there is no reason to be overly concerned at this time. But the satellites indicate that Tropical Storm Suzy has strengthened and changed directions. Yesterday, it appeared that the storm would continue on its path up the Atlantic and not hit land. However, it is now heading west toward Jamaica, and if it continues to strengthen on its current path, there is a small but growing chance that the storm will be upgraded to a hurricane, and we could be impacted. We will continue to update you as soon as we know more, so stay tuned."

My mother lowered the volume and tossed the remote on a chair. She seemed puzzled as she glanced around at her guests.

"Tropical Storm Suzy?" Josie said, laughing.

"I guess they heard you were coming for a visit," Chef Claire said, laughing along.

"Shut it. Mom, I thought hurricane season was over."

"It is," my mother said. "What do you think Gerald?"

"I have to say I'm perplexed," he said. "I heard a report earlier today about a tropical storm, but I didn't give it a second thought."

"Has there ever been a hurricane here in December?" Josie said.

"No, I don't think so," Gerald said. "But there have obviously been some big storms."

"The way the weather is these days, it's really not that surprising, right?" Bill said. "We've certainly done a good job messing up the climate."

"I guess anything's possible," Gerald said.

A big gust of wind rattled the windows, and we heard the sound of palms slapping the side of the house.

"Okay," my mother said, heading for the verandah. "Time to batten down the hatches. Henry, can you please give me a hand with the storm shutters?"

"Of course," Henry said, following my mother.

"I hate to do this, but it's probably a good idea for you folks to head home," my mother said. "Just to be on the safe side."

Everyone quickly gathered their belongings, said goodbye to each other, then headed out the front door. We offered our help, but my mother waved us away, and we watched as she and Henry efficiently went about the job of lowering and locking the storm shutters that wrapped around the outside of the verandah.

Five minutes later, the doorbell rang. I opened it and saw all of the dinner guests standing in the doorway. They were wind-blown and drenched. I motioned them in, and they quickly stepped inside and huddled in the foyer.

"What's going on?" I said, confused.

"The wind knocked down two giant palm trees, and they're laying across the driveway. I don't think anybody is going anywhere tonight," Gerald said.

My mother and Henry came in and closed the verandah door behind them. Gerald explained what had happened and my mother listened carefully then shrugged.

"Well, then I guess we'll just have a pajama party and ride out the storm," she said "Henry, I think we have a ton of casual wear in the pantry closet. Why don't you go find some towels and dry clothes for our guests while I sort out the sleeping arrangements?"

I watched my mother with a touch of pride as she calmly handled the situation with an efficient precision she always managed to summon when needed. She again refused our help, and I was about to sit down to get a weather update when a thought popped into my head as I reached for the remote.

"Oh, no," I said, staring at Josie.

"You're right," she said. "We need to do something."

"What is it?" Chef Claire said.

"The bloodhound," we said in unison.

Chapter 6

My mother gave me her best *don't you dare defy me* look. I did my best to ignore her as Josie and I rummaged through the garage.

"Are you listening to me, young lady?"

I flinched when I got the always dangerous *young lady* but continued looking through a large box of assorted junk.

"Suzy Chandler," my mother snapped. "Look at me when I'm talking to you."

"I'm a little busy at the moment, Mom," I said, grabbing two pieces of rope and tossing them into a backpack.

"I forbid you two to go outside in this weather."

"Aren't you the one who was always telling me to go outside and play?" I said, giving her a crocodile smile she did not appreciate.

"We'll be fine, Mrs. C.," Josie said. "It's just a little wind and rain."

"Exactly," I said, grabbing two flashlights and testing them to make sure they worked. "And it's not that far up the beach. We'll be back before you know it."

"I'll make sure to wave as you blow by," my mother said. "You two are such a pain sometimes."

"Yes, I'm sure we are, Mom," I said, giving her a quick peck on the cheek as I walked past her. "But it keeps you young, right?"

"You're going to risk life and limb for a dog? A stray dog you just happened to see on the beach?"

Josie and I glanced at each other, then back at my mother.

"Well, yeah," we said in unison.

"You're a couple of idiots," she said, storming back into the house.

"You know, she's probably right," Josie said, grabbing a blanket and stuffing it into the backpack she was holding.

"We'll deal with that later," I said, pulling the backpack over my shoulders. "Are you ready?"

"Let's go," Josie said, heading for the door that led outside to the pool area. "Oh, and Suzy?"

"Yeah?"

"It was nice knowing you," Josie deadpanned on her way out.

I followed her outside, and we hunkered down against the wind and rain and made our way along the path that led to the beach. We stayed on the upper edge of the sand as far away as possible from the water. The waves were already reaching halfway up the beach, and the wind whipped a constant spray of mist as we struggled through the ankle-high sand.

"This sucks," Josie yelled over the wind.

"Yeah, it kinda does. Just try to remember one thing," I yelled back.

"What's that?"

"You're on vacation."

"Is this the part where you tell me the glass is half-full?"

"Not for long if it keeps raining like this."

"Funny," she said, grabbing my arm for balance.

"What do we do if he's not there?"

"We go back."

Unable to find fault with her logic, I nodded to myself as I trudged up the beach.

It took us a lot longer than I'd hoped, and by the time we made it to the spot where we'd seen the bloodhound earlier, I was puffing and wheezing like a smoker with a three pack a day habit and one lung. I bent at the knees and struggled to get air into my lungs. Eventually, I stood up and fought back the urge to throw up.

"I really need to get to the gym," I gasped.

"This is sort of like a trip to the gym," Josie said, breathing heavily as rainwater poured off her. She scanned the immediate area with her flashlight then focused the beam on a nearby house. "I think this is the one we saw this afternoon. Let's head up to the lawn and go from there."

I managed a small nod and followed her as she left the beach. I felt the wet grass on my bare feet, and we came to a stop and again swept our flashlights back and forth. Then I caught a glimpse of something moving through the palms in front of us.

"There he is," I said, focusing the light on the bloodhound.

"Where the heck is he going?" Josie said. "No, he's stopped. No, wait. He's watching us and pacing back and forth."

"It looks like he's trying to get us to follow him," I said, frowning. "Do you think he wants to show us something?"

"You mean like Lassie?"

"Well, I doubt if anybody has fallen down a well," I said, frowning.

"What?" Josie said, shining the light in my eyes.

"Somebody was always falling down a well on that show."

"Will you forget about Lassie?"

"You're the one who brought it up," I said, waving the beam of light away from my face.

We refocused on the bloodhound that was keeping a very close eye on us.

"Okay, I think I've got it figured out," Josie said. "He doesn't want us to follow him so he can show us something."

"He doesn't?" I said, pointing my flashlight at her face.

She didn't like it any more than I did, and she grimaced and turned her head.

"No, he wants us to follow him, so we won't see something he's trying to hide."

"And you know this how?"

"Let's call it my gut instincts as a vet," she said, shrugging.

"Whatever," I said, cringing as another strong gust of wind hammered us. "What doesn't he want us to see?"

"He's protecting something," Josie said. "And my guess it's another dog. Or maybe a momma and her puppies."

"Out here in this weather?"

"Well, if they're strays, where are they gonna go?"

"Good point," I said, nodding. "How do you want to play it?"

"Well, first we need to make sure we don't get bit," Josie said.

"Yeah, that would be a good start. Let's split up. You're the dog Svengali, so you handle the bloodhound. I'll go see what I can find hidden in the bushes over by those palms."

"Got it," Josie said, lowering the flashlight beam as she began heading straight for the bloodhound.

I watched and heard the dog growl and take a step toward Josie.

"Easy, easy," Josie cooed as she continued to slowly work her way across the wet grass. "Easy does it, big guy."

The growling intensified, but Josie kept moving forward talking just loud enough to be heard over the storm. When she was three feet away, she extended her arm, and the dog stopped growling long enough to take a whiff.

"Good boy," Josie said, then gestured for me to get on with my search.

I slowly worked my way across the lawn, and the bloodhound trotted in my direction and let loose with a low growl.

"Okay, I think we're onto something," Josie said, slowly working her way toward me. "He's definitely trying to protect something. Hold out your hand and let him sniff you."

"Swimming with the stingrays is starting to look pretty good," I said, extending my arm toward the dog.

"What?"

"Never mind. Not important," I said, doing my best to hold my arm still.

The dog inched closer and sniffed my hand. I reached out to pet him, and he jumped back a few feet.

"Easy, big boy," Josie said, approaching from the other side. "Good dog."

She extended her hand and gently placed it on the bloodhound's head. The dog stiffened, but relaxed when she began scratching his ear. Eventually, the dog sat down on the grass and let loose with a soft, plaintive wail.

"He's scared," Josie said, kneeling down to hug the dog. "No collar. Good boy, who's a good boy, that's it, easy does it."

The dog nestled his head against her and licked her hand.

"How on earth do you do that?" I said, once again baffled by her abilities.

"I speak dog, remember?" she said, gently patting the dog on the back and slipping a piece of rope over his head. "Okay, let's go see what we can find."

Josie led the dog to me, and I rubbed his head and received a couple of hand licks in return. The bloodhound started moving toward the shrubs and pulled Josie along as the rope tightened. Moments later, he stopped in front of a small section of grass that was partially hidden by the shrubs. I shined the beam down and found myself staring into the saddest pair of eyes I'd seen in a long time.

"Oh, it's a basset hound," I said, kneeling down next to her. "And look at these little guys."

"They're gorgeous," Josie said, sitting down on the grass. "It looks like there's six of them. They're around five or six weeks I think."

Josie continued to hug and pet the bloodhound as I stroked the basset's head. She looked scared and exhausted which was completely understandable since she was stuck outside in a major storm trying to take care of six hungry puppies.

"Let's get them back to the house," I said, then frowned. "How the heck are we gonna do that?"

"That's a very good question," Josie said. "We can use the rope for leads on mom and pop, but we'll have to figure out a way to carry the puppies."

"Yeah, there's no way they're gonna be able to walk," I said. "Hang on, I got an idea."

"I can't wait to hear it," Josie said as the rain continued to pour off her head.

"We can connect the two backpacks together and use it as a carry sling. And we can put the blankets down on top for the puppies."

"Great idea. We can walk side by side, and hold one end of the sling, and walk mom and pop with our other hand."

"You think they'll let us move the puppies?" I said.

"There's only one way to find out," Josie said, stroking the bloodhound's head.

I sat down on the wet grass next to her, and we quickly assembled the makeshift sling. We tucked the blankets in the best we could then looked at each other.

"You ready?" Josie said.

"To get bit? Not really. But I guess we don't have a choice."

I leaned over to pet mama, then gently lifted the first puppy that was soaked and trembling with fear. I placed her down on the sling, and the basset stared at me but remained relatively calm. I slowly repeated the process with the rest of the puppies, then gently slipped a piece of rope over the basset's head.

"Are you guys ready to go for a walk?" I said, sliding onto my knees.

Josie stood and waited for me. When I was on my feet, we reached down and grabbed one end of the sling and lifted. The puppies glanced around nervously but seemed to enjoy the feel of the warm blankets and stayed right where they were. We took a coordinated step toward the house and held our breath that mom and pop would follow suit. Whether they trusted us, or simply wanted to get out of the storm, they walked alongside us as we struggled down the beach fighting the wind and rain the whole way. Every few steps, the adult dogs snuck glances at the sling to make sure the puppies were safe, but, eventually, they seemed even more determined to get out of the storm than we were. As such, they were pulling us along the last hundred yards, and we finally hit the path that led up to my mother's house.

As we made our way up the path, a beam of light hit us, and we froze in our tracks.

"Who's there?" I said, pointing my flashlight back at the incoming beam.

"It's me."

"Henry?" I said as Josie and I resumed our exhausting trek up the path.

"Yes, it's me," Henry said, walking toward us. "What do you have there?"

"Just a few more houseguests," Josie said. "What are you doing outside?"

"The power went off, and I need to start the generator.

I glanced at the house and noticed it was in total darkness.

"I thought something looked different when we were coming up the path," I said to Josie.

"Oh, stop it. You missed it completely, and you know it," Josie said, laughing.

"Shut it. Let's get these guys inside."

"I'll see you in a few minutes," Henry said, giving us a quick wave as he headed for a small shed.

My mother must have been on the lookout for the beams from our flashlights because she opened the door while we were still making our way across the lawn. When she saw what we had with us, she shook her head and ushered us inside. We gently set the sling down on the garage floor and removed the makeshift leads from the bloodhound and basset.

"You two are something else," she said, handing us both towels.

We both quickly wiped our faces, then started drying the dogs.

Then we heard the surprisingly comforting sound of a diesel engine coming to life over the roar of the wind, and the lights came back on.

Just as I was about to bend down to get my first good look at the dogs, all three of us froze when we heard a blood-curdling scream coming from inside the house.

Chapter 7

We made sure the dogs were settled in with dry blankets and water, then followed my mother inside the house. When we reached the living room, we glanced around at the shocked expressions on everyone's face, and it was clear that something bad had happened that justified the scream. I made eye contact with Chef Claire who was sitting in a chair by herself and motioned for her to come closer. She walked over with tears in her eyes and exhaled loudly.

"What on earth is the matter with everybody?" I said, glancing around the room.

"That," Chef Claire said, nodding toward the hallway on the other side of the living room that led to the bedrooms.

Josie and I took a step forward then noticed Wily Smith sitting on the floor with his back against the wall and his legs splayed in front of him.

"Drunk?" I said to Chef Claire.

"Look closer," she said, wiping her eyes with the back of her hand.

I did, then jumped back startled when I saw the metal skewer sticking out of his chest. A collection of grilled tomatoes and mushrooms was scattered on the floor directly in front of him.

"Dead?" I said.

"Very," Chef Claire said, nodding.

"Really?" Josie said, looking up at the heavens. "Another one? Are you freaking kidding me?"

"He got killed with a skewer?" I said, baffled by the notion.

"Well, I doubt if it was the grilled vegetables," Josie said.

"Don't start," I said, glaring at her.

"I was merely making a point," she said. "We heard a scream when we were in the garage."

"That was me," Chef Claire said. "When the lights came back on, he was right in front of where I was sitting."

"You got a set of lungs on you," Josie said. "Okay, Detective Snoop, what's the plan?"

"Well, I was going to spend the rest of the night playing with the puppies, but I guess that's off the table."

"You got puppies?" Chef Claire said.

"Yes, six of the most gorgeous bloodhound and basset mix you'll ever see," Josie said.

"And they're in the garage?" Chef Claire said.

"Yeah. You're going to love them," I said.

My mother cleared her throat and glared at us. Chastised like a group of schoolgirls, we fell silent and stood at attention as we waited for her to address the group.

"I don't know what to say," my mother said. "This is obviously a horrible tragedy and Prunella, from all of us, please accept our deepest sympathy for your loss. Geez, this is extremely difficult."

My mother paused and waited for the sobbing Prunella to find her bearings. The rest of the group continued to exchange looks and sneak peeks at the dead body sitting underneath a painting of my mother's house that was signed by Sky. I watched my mother struggle with the situation.

"I don't think I've ever seen your mom at a loss for words," Josie said.

"Give her a minute," I said, studying my mother. "She'll find her feet in a sec."

"Okay, first things first," my mother said. "Gerald, if you can get cell reception, please call the police and let them know what's happened. I'm not sure if they'll be able to get out here tonight given this storm, but we need to report it."

"Of course," Gerald said, grabbing his phone as he headed for the kitchen.

"Next, we'll need to do something with the body," my mother said, grimacing at the death stare Wily was giving her.

"I guess we could stick him out on the verandah," Bill from Buffalo said.

"Or the garage," Henry said, glancing around.

"We'll have to move the dogs first," Josie said.

"What dogs?" Jerry said.

"The eight dogs in the garage," Josie said.

"Eight?" Bill said. "Where the hell did eight dogs come from?"

"From the beach," Josie said. "They're gorgeous."

"Will you people forget about the dogs?" Prunella said. "Let's try to focus on my dead husband, okay?"

The room fell silent except for a fresh round of sobs coming from the grieving widow.

"Uh, Mom?"

"Yes, darling."

"You can't move the body," I said, softly. "This is a murder scene."

Prunella wailed when she heard my comment, and Bill and Jerry tried consoling her on the couch. Soon, her cries were replaced by soft sobbing, and my mother continued.

"Yes, of course, darling. You're absolutely right," my mother said, frowning as she looked at the body that was partially blocking the hallway. "Well, we'll just have to be careful when we're walking past Wily. We need to keep our distance to make sure we don't tamper with any evidence. Or step in any blood."

"That's not gonna be a problem," Josie whispered.

"Shut it," I said.

"What else?" my mother said out loud to herself. "Oh, my...how do I say this?" She exhaled then shrugged and continued. "Since it's pretty obvious that this wasn't an accident, it means that the person who stabbed Wily is in the room right now."

That comment definitely got everyone's attention, including mine, and I found myself looking around the room trying to read the facial expression of everyone I made eye contact with.

"As soon as we hear what Gerald has to say, we'll figure out our next steps," my mother said, sneaking another peek at the dead body. "And until we have a better idea of what might be going on, please take any precautions you feel are necessary. I can't believe I'm saying this, but you might want to lock your bedroom door tonight when you retire."

An eerie murmur filled the room as everyone began pondering what my mother had said. Then several whispered conversations ensued as people began discussing their options.

"Perhaps those of you who plan on staying up would be interested in joining me in the great room. We could play cards, and I believe we have quite a collection of board games."

"I could go for a good game of Clue," Josie deadpanned in a whisper.

Chef Claire and I stifled snorts of laughter that generated another glare from my mother.

"Sorry, Mom," I whispered.

"I'm going to go play with the dogs," Chef Claire said.

"Now, there's an idea," Josie said.

Rolling around on the floor with a bunch of puppies sounded a whole lot better than trying to figure out who killed the philandering financier with a skewer of grilled vegetables, and I followed Chef Claire and Josie into the garage even as my Snoopmeter redlined.

Chapter 8

Deciding that the dogs deserved better than being stuck in the garage all by themselves, we brought all eight inside into the kitchen. Josie and I cut leftover steak and chicken into small pieces and filled bowls for the bloodhound and the basset. It was obvious they hadn't been eating well of late, and they quickly downed their dinner and sniffed the air for more. The puppies were also on the prowl, and I looked at Josie.

"What do you think?" I said.

"Well, they're certainly old enough for solid food," Josie said. "But let's not overdo it. Let's stick with the chicken and make sure to cut it into small pieces. And let's feed them by hand so we can keep a close eye on how much each one is eating. It's probably their first solid food, and it might upset their little tummies."

"I have to hand-feed a bunch of puppies?" I said as I started cutting a chicken breast. "Oh, no, not the briar patch."

We sat on the cool tile floor and fed all six puppies then watched them playfully attack and torment each other as the protein kicked in. We tried to forget about the dead guy I assumed was starting to stiffen with rigor mortis and focus on our new friends. The bloodhound had bonded with Josie and wouldn't leave her side. Mama kept a close eye on her puppies as they rolled around on the kitchen floor, but occasionally snuck me a sad-eyed look that made me melt. Chef Claire was stretched out in the middle of the floor with the puppies and beaming as they climbed over her.

Thirty minutes later, the puppies were worn out and sound asleep. Gerald entered the kitchen and stopped when he saw the dogs sprawled out on the floor.

"Now, there's a sight," he said, laughing as he opened the fridge to grab a beer.

"Any news from the police?" I said.

"I finally got through to them," he said, taking a sip. "But there are trees down all over, and the power is still out in town. So, I seriously doubt if they're going to be able to make it out here tonight."

"Couldn't they get here by coming up the beach?" Josie said.

"No, between the wind and the storm surge, they're really not sure what they'd be dealing with. And I imagine they have a lot to keep an eye on in town. So, I guess we're on our own until morning."

"Well, it's not like Wily is going anywhere," I said, shrugging.

Josie and Chef Claire both glanced at me and nodded their assent.

"I must say that all three of you are handling this very calmly," Gerald said.

"I guess practice makes perfect," I said, shrugging again.

"You've been around a murder scene before?" he said, confused.

"Oh, yeah. Seven over the past several months," I said, casually.

"Seven?" Gerald said, now baffled.

"No, it was more than seven," Josie said. "Some of the cases involved more than one murder."

"Well, sure," I said. "I was just counting cases."

"Seven murder cases?" Gerald said. "I thought you ran an inn for dogs."

"We do," I said. "But something always seems to come up. I'm sure you know how that goes."

"I can't say that I do," he said, sitting down in a chair. "Do tell."

"Well, let's see," I said, searching my memory bank. "There was the candy magnate who overdosed and drowned."

"That's when we first met Chef Claire," Josie said.

"Bacon wrapped chili dogs," I said, smiling at Chef Claire. "I'll never forget them."

"And then I got arrested for murder," Chef Claire said.

"Really?" Gerald said. "They thought you killed this candy magnate?"

"No, they thought I killed his ex-wife. But I ended up getting off."

"That was one of the cases with multiple murders," Josie said.

"Yeah," I said. "I almost forgot about her. What was her name?"

"Marge," Chef Claire said.

"That's right," I said. "What a piece of work she was."

Gerald shifted in his seat as he listened to us.

"Remember how bloated that guy was?" Josie said.

"That's not something you can easily forget," I said. "He looked like he was about to explode."

"From the chili dogs?" Gerald said.

"No, from the water and the maple syrup," Josie said.

"Yeah, that was disgusting," I said, frowning.

"Maple syrup?" Gerald said, rubbing his forehead.

"Yeah, it was pretty weird. Then there was the guy on the yacht," Josie said. "And the boat captain that got his head squished between the boat and the dock."

"Ew, don't remind me," I said.

Gerald sat quietly staring at us in disbelief.

"Then there was the guy who froze to death in the phone booth," Chef Claire said.

"I think he got shot first, didn't he?" I said.

"Yeah, maybe," Josie said with a frown. "But I can't remember. They all tend to blur together after a while."

"No, he definitely got shot first," I said. "Remember when we found him frozen stiff as a board, he already had that huge hole in his forehead?"

"Oh, you're right. And then the Baxter Brothers disappeared right around the same time," Josie said.

"The Baxter Brothers?" Gerald said.

"Dognappers who eventually washed up on shore dead," I said. "Long story."

"Let's see, there's been a couple of stabbings, some more gunshots, and, of course, the mob guy who overdosed on his houseboat," Chef Claire said.

"Mob guy?" Gerald said, staring at Chef Claire.

"Jimmy Calducci," Josie said.

"Yeah. And don't forget Fatal Franny," I said, smiling.

"Fatal Franny?" Gerald said, glancing around at us.

"She did contract hits for Calducci," Josie said. "Wasn't that the time you almost spent the night in the freezer?"

"That was the one," I said, then looked at Gerald. "Then there was Buggy and the bank robbery."

"Buggy? Who the heck is Buggy?" Gerard said.

"He was from a wealthy family, but he got banished and ended up on the street," I said, shaking my head. "That one would take all night to tell."

"Caspian the Goth Geisha Girl artist," Chef Claire said, chuckling.

"I liked her," I said.

"Don't forget the old woman matriarch," Josie said.

"Hated her," I said.

"And we can't forget Roxanne, the former girlfriend of the dead candy magnate's gardener who ended up married to Buggy's brother," Chef Claire said.

"She was quite the gold digger," I explained to Gerald. "Josie ended up stabbing her."

"What?" he said, staring at Josie.

"That was an accident, and you know it," Josie snapped.

"Who are you people?" Gerald said.

"Let's see. What else?" I said. "Oh yeah, most recently we had to deal with Rooster's cousin, Coke Bottle, who stole Al and Dente."

"Coke Bottle stole Al and Dente?"

"Yes," Josie said. "Can you believe that? And then two people got run over by the dog judge when they were crossing the street."

"But we weren't around to see the hit and run happen," Chef Claire said.

"Yeah, Suzy had to piece that one together from a distance," Josie said. "That was pretty amazing to watch."

"Why, thank you," I said, flashing her a quick smile before refocusing on Gerald. "So, I guess you can see why we're handling the situation with Wily a bit different from what you might expect."

"Would I be correct assuming that you'll be trying to *piece together* what happened here tonight?" Gerald said, getting to his feet.

"Well, I'm supposed to be on vacation," I said. "So, I'd rather not if at all possible. For now, my plan is to sit here and play with mama and papa and their six little ones."

I smiled as I glanced down at the puppies, then frowned and scanned the kitchen floor.

"Uh-oh," I said, standing up.

"What's the matter?" Josie said.

"I only see five puppies."

"Oh, no," Josie said, climbing to her feet and following me out of the kitchen.

We found the missing puppy down the hall having a great time as he rolled around on his back in the pool of blood that had collected between Wily's legs.

"So much for the crime scene," I said, bending down to scoop the puppy up.

Wide awake and ready to play, the puppy gently pawed at my face and nuzzled its head against my chest.

"Somebody needs a bath," I said, rubbing the puppy's head as I headed for the garage. "How bad do I look?"

"Do you remember the prom scene from Carrie?"

"Still not funny."

Chapter 9

I gently hosed the blood off the puppy, then soaped her up with liquid dish detergent I'd found in the kitchen, rinsed her off, and dried her with a towel. As I was doing that, Josie and Chef Claire built a doggy bed out of blankets and pillows that looked comfy enough to climb into. The basset climbed up onto the makeshift bed and kept a close eye on her puppies. Soon, the puppies, one by one, nestled up against her and drifted off. The bloodhound supervised until he was satisfied that all was well with the world, then stretched out behind the basset hound and stared at Josie.

"You've made a new friend," I said, nodding at the bloodhound.

"He's a great dog. Okay," Josie said, taking the puppy out of my arms. "She's clean. Your turn."

I headed to my bedroom to shower and change clothes. I veered around Wily's legs as I made my way down the hallway, and started to remove my blood-stained tee shirt that was beginning to stick to my skin. I pulled the shirt back down when I heard a noise coming from the first bedroom on the right.

Remembering that I would probably be spending the night trapped in a house with a killer, I slowed down as I passed the bedroom and listened closely. But the only thing I could hear was the muffled conversation of two people, so I continued to my room, locked the door behind me, and hopped into the shower.

It wasn't quite the shower scene from Carrie, but there was more than enough blood to get my attention, and I was glad it wasn't mine. I toweled off, changed into my sweats, then headed back down the hall. The sounds coming from the bedroom had changed. The muffled conversation had been replaced by the grunts and groans of two people who were either getting reacquainted or getting to know each other very well for the first time. I scurried past the bedroom door and made a mental note to check out who was missing when I found the rest of the group.

I headed for the great room, a well-named, high-ceilinged section of the house that was strewn with several sitting areas comprised of overstuffed chairs and couches. A half dozen ceiling fans gently rotated above, and I enjoyed the breeze they were producing as I looked around. Chef Claire and Josie were sitting on a couch with their feet on a coffee table and sipping wine. Directly across from them, Jerry was stretched out on another couch reading a book. Sitting around a circular card table were my mother and Gerald, Bill, and Thomas, the banker who I'd barely said a word to all evening.

I stood behind my mother who tossed a handful of chips into the pot and spoke to me without turning around.

"Call," my mother said. "What's up, darling?"

"Where's everybody else?"

"I imagine they've all turned in," she said, studying the table. "You're going to raise me, Thomas? That's very brave of you."

"Not when you consider the hand I'm holding," Thomas said, puffing on a large cigar.

"Too rich for my blood," Bill said, folding.

"Me too," Gerald said, laughing. "After all, I'm just a poor government servant."

"Yeah," my mother said, giving Gerald a coy smile. "And I'm Peter Pan."

"I heard noises coming from one of the bedrooms," I whispered into my mother's ear.

"Good for you, darling," she said, then glanced over her shoulder. "What kind of noises?"

"It was the sound of...you know, two people getting busy," I said.

"From a bedroom?" she said, shaking her head. "I'm shocked."

"Mom. Don't start."

"Darling, in case you're forgotten, it's quite a common occurrence in the bedroom. Now, if you don't mind, I'm about two hands away from winning Thomas's Bentley."

"What the heck would you do with a Bentley?" I said, frowning.

"It's the principle of the thing," she said, drawing two cards.

"Aren't you the least bit worried about what might happen the rest of the evening?"

"Darling, I've got a dead body with a vacant stare leaving blood stains all over my Italian tile. And I'm trapped in my own house with the person who did it. I don't think this evening could get much worse."

"Unless the killer decides to do it again," I whispered, then smiled back at the annoyed looks I was getting from the rest of the card players.

"Don't be silly," she said. "Whoever killed Wily had him specifically in mind."

"And you know this how?"

"Let's call it local knowledge and leave it at that," my mother said as she tossed another stack of chips into the pot. "Reraise."

"I can't believe it," Thomas said, tossing his cards away. "What did you have?"

"Sorry, Thomas," my mother said, grinning as she pulled the chips toward her. "But you gotta pay to see my cards." She glanced over her shoulder again. "Will there be anything else, darling?"

"No, I'm done here."

"Try and get some sleep. You'll need to be fresh in the morning for the police," she said, stacking her chips. "Whose turn is it to deal?"

I wandered back to where Josie and Chef Claire were sitting and sat down in a chair near Jerry's couch.

"What are you reading?" I said.

"Agatha Christie," Jerry said. "Ten Little Indians."

"Perfect," I said, shaking my head.

"What's the book about?" Chef Claire said.

"You're not familiar with Ten Little Indians? It's one of the bestselling books of all time," Josie said. "Don't you read murder mysteries?"

"I live with you two," Chef Claire said. "Why bother?"

"Redundant, huh?" Josie said, taking a sip of wine.

"To say the least," Chef Claire said. "So, what's it about?"

"It's about a group of people who are invited to a remote island, and they end up getting stuck there and are unable to escape due to inclement weather. Gradually, all ten are killed off one by one."

"I was walking past the bookcase when I saw it. For some reason, I just had to grab it and start reading. Weird, huh?" Jerry said.

"Weird's a word for it," I said.

Jerry sat up and leaned closer. "Who do you think killed Wily?"

"I've got it narrowed down to a dozen suspects," I said.

"Really?" Jerry thought about it, then frowned. "Hang on. Not counting you, there are only a dozen people here."

"I like to start with the widest circle of suspects possible."

"You really are funny," Jerry said, chuckling as she stretched out and got back to her book.

"Don't encourage her," Josie said, then nodded at me. "Detective Snoop. I'd like a word with you."

I followed her to another sitting area out of earshot of the others and sat down across from her.

"What's up?" I said.

"What were you whispering to your mother about?" Josie said.

"I told her that I heard two people in one of the bedrooms," I said. "You know, they were…"

"Yeah. Got it," Josie said, glancing around. "This shouldn't be that hard to figure out. I guess we can start by ruling you out."

"Why? Because my love life is a total disaster?"

"Actually, I was going to say because you're sitting right across from me, but we can go with disastrous love life if you like," she deadpanned.

"Shut it," I said. "We're missing five people. Henry, Sky, and Timothy. And two of the women. Prunella and Sally."

"Interesting," Josie said.

"Why's that?"

"Because no matter what combination you use, none of those five are involved with each other," Josie said.

"At least publicly."

"Nothing gets past you," Josie said, grinning.

"Hey, I'm supposed to be on vacation," I said, glaring at her. "According to Gerald, Sally has quite the reputation as a player."

"Interesting. Did he say anything about Prunella?"

"The widow? No, not really. But I can't imagine she'd be in the mood at the moment given the condition her husband is in."

"Yeah, I suppose," Josie said. "Unless she was involved in the murder. Maybe she did it, got an adrenaline rush, and is in there with a friend trying to take the edge off."

"Possible," I said, nodding. "According to Gerald, Wily was also a major player."

"That doesn't surprise me. He kept staring at me during dinner. It totally creeped me out."

"Yeah, I noticed. What did you learn about the painter?"

"Sky? Well, for one, I learned that he paints a lot more than just landscapes."

"Let me guess. He does artistic nudes for his own private collection and would just love to paint you?"

"There she is. There's the Detective Snoop I know," she said, laughing. "He promised me it would be tastefully done and our little secret."

"Yuk. So Sky goes on the list of suspects."

"Yeah, for now anyway," Josie said. "What about that guy who was boring you to death earlier?"

"Timothy. I wasn't paying close attention so, apart from learning how boring he is, I didn't get a good read on him."

"Do you think Henry and your mom are an item?"

"I don't think so," I said, shaking my head. "They're obviously good friends, but he works for her. And that's just not my mom's style."

"Then there's no reason for him not to be in the bedroom with someone else," Josie said.

"I guess not. I'm not even sure why I fixated on it. Two people hooking up probably doesn't have anything to do with the murder."

"I'm not sure. Most of the time we seem to be looking at either money or jealousy as the motive, right?"

"What about it?" I said.

"Well, it's pretty clear that these people have way more than enough money."

"They'd probably disagree with you, but I take your point," I said. "I guess jealousy is as good as anything to go on for the moment."

"Yeah," Josie said, then sighed.

"What?"

"There goes our vacation."

"Maybe. But we did good rescuing the dogs."

"Yes, we sure did," Josie said, grinning. "Oh, I asked your mom if she knew if there was an animal shelter around. Turns out, there's one not far from here."

"That's great. As soon as we can get out of here, let's go check it out."

"If it doesn't get blown away by this storm," Josie said.

Chapter 10

The wind and rain continued all night, but the storm never reached hurricane level. I wasn't sure what it would have taken for it to meet the official definition, and I was glad I wasn't forced to find out. I woke early, stretched and yawned, made a quick bathroom stop, then headed straight for the garage. Josie and Chef Claire were already there sipping coffee.

"Morning," I said, accepting Chef Claire's mug from her. "Thanks. How are these guys doing?"

"Apart from the expected accidents over by the door, they're doing great," Josie said, petting the bloodhound who was following her around stride for stride.

We waited out another extended gust of wind and heard the rain continue to pound down. I sat down on the makeshift dog bed and stroked the basset's head and began playing with the puppies who were doing their best to get their breakfast out of mama.

"She must be starting to dry up," Josie said. "I think we should get them on solid food and keep them there."

"If we can ever get out of here to buy some dog food," I said.

"There's a ton of steak and chicken in the freezer," Chef Claire. "Your mom won't mind, will she?"

"No, not in the least," I said.

"So, what's the plan for today, Snoopmeister?" Josie said.

"Well, I thought we'd start by throwing a sheet over the body. It's creeping me out."

"Somebody should have done that last night," Chef Claire said.

"We were trying to preserve the crime scene, but then somebody went and ruined it," I said, gently rolling the guilty puppy over onto his back. "Didn't you?"

The puppy stared up at me, then kicked his legs playfully and snorted. I removed my hand, and he rolled over then climbed up on my chest and nuzzled me. The door leading into the house opened, and my mother stuck her head through the opening.

"Good morning, ladies," she said. "Henry has made pancakes."

"Great," Josie said. "I'm starved."

"Mom, can I have a word with you?"

"Of course, darling," she said, stepping inside then sliding to one side to let Chef Claire and Josie get past her. "What's up?"

"I just wanted to get your take on what happened to Wily."

"It's pretty clear *what* happened to him, so I assume you'd like my opinion about who might have done it," she said, bending down to pet a couple of the puppies. "Cute dogs. I think your love of dogs is finally starting to wear off on me."

"It took you long enough," I whispered.

"What?"

"Nothing. Who do you think did it?"

"I really can't say, darling."

"Don't know or can't say?"

"Exactly."

"Mom."

"I'm sorry," she said, grinning at me. "You're supposed to be on vacation. Why don't you just relax and let the police handle this one?"

"You know me better than that."

"Yes, I'm afraid I do," she said, stuffing her hands into her back pockets as she glanced around the garage. "I really need to repaint out here."

"Mom."

"Okay, darling. Relax. While I'm not sure who killed Wily, I will say he's been sticking his nose where it doesn't belong lately and making life difficult for some of the people around him."

"Because of his philandering, right?"

"Sure, let's go with that," she said, nodding.

"That's not the reason?" I said, frowning.

"Let's say that it could have been part of the equation," she said, casually glancing around. "Yes, repainting is definitely the way to go."

"Why are you being so evasive about this, Mom?"

"Evasive? I believe I've answered all your questions, darling. What do you think about a light blue? Or maybe an off-white? It's always such a hard decision. And I'm always looking for one coat coverage."

I stared at her as she continued to glance around the garage. Then a lightbulb went off in my head.

"I think you might want to go with a darker color, Mom."

"Really? That's interesting," she said, slowly nodding.

"Yeah, something a bit darker is probably the way to go," I said, studying her reaction closely. "After all, you want to make sure that you completely cover up all the imperfections."

"That's my girl," she said, beaming at me.

Chapter 11

Even Chef Claire was impressed by the quality of Henry's pancakes, and we gorged ourselves, helped clean up, then headed for the garage. But before we got out of the kitchen, my mother stopped us in our tracks with a look and a nod toward the living room where the rest of the guests had wandered after breakfast. I was pleased to see the sheet draped over the corpse that was still resting against the wall underneath the painting. And while the body was in close proximity, the guests had turned their chairs to avoid having to look at it.

We moved one of the couches at a forty-five-degree angle and sat down. I glanced around and tried to get a feel for everyone's mood. Prunella was still distraught and sniffling back tears. She stared off into the distance, audibly sighing whenever her emotions overflowed. The others occasionally patted her back or hugged her and offered soft words of sympathy and encouragement, but for the most part, they left her alone to grieve.

Billy and Jerry from Buffalo sat by themselves holding hands and speaking to each other in hushed tones. Sally was perky, a bit too perky I decided for someone who was fifteen feet away from a dead body. And I was almost certain that she'd been the woman I'd heard in the bedroom last night. Her husband, Thomas, was in a bad mood and pouring copious amounts of brandy into his morning coffee. Either he had learned of his wife's indiscretion, or my mother had, in fact, won his Bentley from him playing cards. Gerald was sitting off by himself making one phone call after another. His mood never seemed to change despite whatever he was being told on the other end of the line, and he casually nibbled pieces of fruit and cheese as he chatted.

Sky, the landscape artist, spotted Josie, and he started to make his way toward us. On his way past Sally, he brushed against her and gently squeezed her hand. She patted his thigh then turned away to study one of the paintings on the wall.

"Perv alert," I said, nudging both of them with an elbow.

"Great," Josie said, shaking her head.

He pulled up a chair across from our couch and sat down.

"I take it you ladies all slept well," he said to all of us but staring at Josie. "I know I did."

I wondered if Sally has been the primary reason for his restful night.

"I did," Josie said. "How about you, Chef Claire?"

"I've slept better," she said. "Suzy?"

"I was a bit restless," I said. "But dead bodies in the hallway always seem to have that effect on me."

Sky flinched then recovered and smiled at me.

"Yes, tragic situation," he whispered. Then he brightened as he turned to Josie. "Have you given my proposal any more thought?"

"You mean the one about me getting naked?" she said with a big smile.

Sky's face reddened, and he cleared his throat. "Well, I wouldn't put it quite that way. It's art. So, what do you think?"

"I think you and Art should stick to landscapes for the rest of the week," Josie said, giving him a cold stare.

"I see," he said, glancing around to look for an escape route.

I noticed Sally sneaking repeated glances our way with a scowl on her face.

"Sky, I hate to bother you," I said. "But would you mind getting me another cup of coffee?"

"I'd love to," he said, jumping out of his chair.

"Well done," Josie said after he was out of earshot.

"It's just way too early in the morning to watch you gut an admirer," I said, yawning.

"What a creep," Chef Claire said.

"Yes," I said, watching Sally as she followed Sky into the kitchen. "But I don't think that opinion is shared by everyone."

Josie and Chef Claire watched Sky place a hand on Sally's lower back as she entered the kitchen. Then they disappeared from view.

"Interesting," Josie said. "Would they have any reason to skewer Wily?"

"Not unless Sally was having a hard time getting rid of him," I said.

"Wily and Sally were an item?" Chef Claire said.

"Gerald said he was pretty sure they used to be, but who knows, right? Maybe Wily had circled back for more and was making life difficult for her."

"And she got Sky to do the dirty work for her?" Chef Claire said.

"Or maybe she took care of Wily herself," I said.

"That's possible," Josie said. "The lights go out, she calls him over, and whispers in his ear to come close and have some more grilled veggies."

Chef Claire snorted coffee all over herself, and I glanced over at Josie.

"Now, that was funny," I said, then something caught my attention. "Listen."

"I don't hear anything," Josie said.

"Exactly. The wind and rain have stopped."

My mother noticed the change in the weather as well, and she and Henry headed for the verandah and raised the storm shutters. The sun was starting to emerge from the clouds, and we walked over to my mother and looked outside.

"What a mess," my mother said, glancing around the lawn strewn with a wide variety of items. "Henry, can you give Carlos a call to see if he can get out here with his crew as soon as possible? And tell him to bring a couple of chainsaws. Those palms blocking the driveway will need to be cut up and hauled away."

"Of course," Henry said, reaching for his phone.

"Well, ladies," my mother said. "What do you feel like doing today?"

"You mean after we talk with the cops, right?" I said.

"Yes, darling. After that."

"We thought we'd head over to the animal shelter," I said.

"Why doesn't that surprise me?" she said, smiling.

"You feel like coming along?"

"I have a couple of conference calls with some folks back home," she said. "Mayoral duties. I'm sure you understand."

"Sure, Mom. Hey, I meant to ask you. How is the town council reacting to the idea of our mayor spending most of the winter down here?"

"With jealousy, primarily," she said, laughing. "Don't worry, darling, I'm not neglecting my official duties. I just don't think I need to be dealing with frostbite while I'm doing them."

Chapter 12

The detective was trying to focus on his line of questioning, but the two puppies circling his feet and nuzzling his ankles kept distracting him. Eventually, he gave up and slipped his pen and notepad into his shirt pocket and bent down to pick both of them up. He held the puppies next to his face, and they began licking him. Whatever level of attraction the three of us already had for the young detective with big muscles and an even bigger smile ratcheted up several levels.

"Gorgeous, and he's a dog lover," Chef Claire whispered.

"Shhh," Josie said.

"So, you two were down on the beach rescuing the dogs when the murder occurred?" the detective said, tucking a puppy under each arm as he looked back and forth at Josie and me.

"I think we were already back here in the garage," I said.

"Yes, that's when we heard Chef Claire's scream coming from inside the house," Josie said.

"And you screamed when you saw the body?"

"She certainly did," Josie said.

"I'm sorry," he said, giving Josie a tight-lipped smile. "But I'm going to need to hear it from her."

"Sorry."

"Yes, I was the one who screamed," Chef Claire said. "I was sitting on a couch next to the couple from Buffalo when the lights went out. And when they came back on, he was the first thing I saw."

"I see. That must have been terrifying for you," the detective said, handing the puppies to me so he could take notes. "And were this couple from Buffalo still sitting next to you when the lights came back on?"

Chef Claire considered the question with a frown.

"Gee, let me think. Yes, I think so. No, maybe not," she said, then shook her head in frustration. "I can't remember. As soon as the people in the room noticed the body, everybody started talking loudly and moving around. I'm sorry, but that part is pretty fuzzy."

"That's okay," he said, beaming at her. "I'm sure it will come to you. And when it does, please call me." He handed her one of his cards. "Actually, feel free to call me even if it doesn't."

"How about that?" I whispered. "He's totally got the hots for her."

"Yeah, and I think she just figured it out," Josie whispered back.

"How can you tell?"

"She's about to bite through her bottom lip."

"Maybe he'll kiss it and make it better."

Josie snorted, and we both flushed red with embarrassment.

"What's that?" the detective said, glancing at me.

"Huh? Oh, I was just saying that, since we weren't around when the murder occurred, you should probably spend some alone time with Chef Claire. She would have much more to offer, and I'm sure you have a lot of questions for her."

"That sounds like a wonderful idea," he said. "Maybe we could have a private chat after I finish up a few things inside."

"Whatever you need, Detective," Chef Claire said. "I'm here for you."

"Perhaps we could do it outside by the pool?" he said.

"Sure."

"Great. Let's say I meet you outside in fifteen minutes?"

"I'll be there."

"I'm looking forward to it," he said, giving her a look that I was sure made her bottom lip bleed. "Ladies, thank you for your time. If I have any other questions, I'll just track you down."

"Don't worry, Detective," Josie said. "You won't have to look very hard."

He waved, gave Chef Claire one more smile, then headed back inside the house.

"I'm here for you?" I said, laughing.

"Shut it," Chef Claire said, red-faced. "Okay, I choked. What can I say?"

"Wow, you got hit hard, girl," Josie said. "How's your lip?"

"I said shut it," Chef Claire said, then exhaled loudly. "I know what you two are up to."

"Yeah," I said. "But I noticed you didn't put up much of a fight."

"Well, he is investigating a murder," Chef Claire said. "I'm just doing my part to help out."

"Of course," I said, nodding.

"How should I play it?" Chef Claire said.

"Well, you've got a week," Josie said. "So, I guess you could take your time for a few days and play it cool, or you could go straight for the jugular."

"This oughta be good," Chef Claire said, folding her arms across her chest.

"Head out to the pool in your bathing suit and take one of the puppies with you," Josie said.

"Now that's not fighting fair," I said, laughing. "The poor guy wouldn't know what hit him."

"But if she wants to make a lasting impact. And she's only got a week," Josie said.

"Good point," I said.

"You two are a big help," Chef Claire said, heading for the door.

"Where are you going?" Josie said.

"To change."

She headed inside, and I let my brain do its thing as I stared off into the distance.

"Uh-oh," Josie said. "Do I smell burning neurons?"

76

"I was just thinking that both of those detectives are very different from what we're used to."

"They're very casual about the whole thing, right?"

"Exactly," I said. "They're asking all the right questions, but they don't seem to be following up or digging into the details."

"Well, we are in the Caymans. And it's definitely way more relaxed down here."

"That could be it," I said. "But it's almost like they really don't care if it gets solved or not."

"That sounds a little harsh."

"Yeah, it probably is," I said, shaking my head. "Still, it seems odd."

"The Finance Minister was here when it happened. Maybe they're just a bit nervous about the politics and have decided to go easy until they get a handle on things."

"Or someone told them to tread lightly."

"Don't start, okay, Suzy? Why don't we stop wondering who stabbed the guy and go see if we can find a good home for some dogs?"

"Why not? After all, we are supposed to be on vacation."

Chapter 13

After the weather had begun to clear, things moved fast. An hour later, the body had been bagged and removed, the palms blocking the driveway had been cut and cleared, the guests had left, and Chef Claire had a dinner date scheduled for later that evening. I approached my mother who was standing on the verandah keeping a close eye on the cleanup efforts on the front lawn and the adjacent stretch of beach. Now that she was no longer playing hostess, she seemed tired and more than a little rattled. I draped an arm around her shoulders and hugged her tight.

"Are you okay, Mom?"

"I'm fine," she said, not taking her eyes off the front lawn.

"You want us to stick around and help out?

"There's really not much to do. Henry is going to scrub the floor where the body was. I'm so glad I decided to go with the tile and not wood."

"Sure, sure."

"And I'm going to handle the breakfast dishes. Apart from that, I think we're fine. You head out and see what you can do about the four-legged creatures who've moved into my garage."

"I'll do that," I said, laughing. "But you have to admit, they are pretty cute."

"Yes, they are, but not cute enough for permanent residence," she said, catching my eye.

"Got it, Mom. Josie and I thought we'd take you and Henry out to dinner tonight."

"That sounds wonderful," she said, nodding. "Won't Chef Claire be joining us?"

"She has a date with that cute detective."

"Really? Well, tell her that she needs to be careful."

"Why's that?"

"From what I understand, he's on a mission to find someone to settle down with. And she has a thing for cops."

"What are you talking about?" I said, frowning. "What thing?"

"For cops. I can't decide if it's because of the uniform, or if it's the safety and protection she believes they provide."

"I've never thought about it. She's always seemed like an equal opportunity dater to me."

"Oh, I'm sure she is. But cops always seem to move right to the head of the line. Remember that FBI agent who showed up the time you accessed that website?"

"Yeah. And for the record, that was an accident."

"Of course, it was just one of those things, right?" she said, smiling as she stared back out at the cleanup efforts. "You saw how Chef Claire reacted when she met him."

"Yes, I did."

I had to give my mother credit. She didn't miss much.

"If he hadn't been transferred back to Washington, I think we would have been seeing a whole lot more of him."

"Well, I'm sure Chef Claire can handle herself."

"Oh, I'm sure of it," my mother said. "But she's starting to get quite restless."

"Restless? No, she's not," I said, shaking my head.

"Yes, she is, darling," my mother said, patting my hand. "You're just choosing not to see it."

"What are you talking about?"

"Chef Claire is different from you and Josie. You've found something you love to do, and the perfect place to do it. And you'd both be happy doing the same thing for the next fifty years."

"What's wrong with that?"

"Absolutely nothing. But Chef Claire is at the point where she's starting to think about her future. You know, wondering is it's time to broaden her horizons a bit."

"What do you mean?"

"She's a world-class chef. As such, she can go anywhere."

"And you're saying that Clay Bay isn't big enough to satisfy her?"

"No, I'm sure it makes her very happy. But perhaps not on a year-round basis."

"You're the one who said that C's had to be open year-round."

"The restaurant, yes," my mother said. "But do you really think that scaled-back winter menu is enough to challenge her? And keep her cooking skills sharp?"

"I guess I never really thought about it."

"And then there's the other thing that's starting to nag at her," my mother said.

"There's more?"

"There's always more, darling. Chef Claire is starting to think about a family. And this isn't a bad place to raise one. At least part of the year."

"Here? In the Caymans?"

"Why not?" my mother said, raising an eyebrow at me.

"But she has a successful restaurant in Clay Bay."

"And I'm the mayor, but I spend most of the winter down here. What's your point, darling?"

"I don't know, Mom," I said, frowning at her. "Right now, I'm having a hard enough time just following the plot."

"I'm just saying that she has options. And perhaps the best way to help her figure out her options and lower her level of stress is by using an *additive* approach."

"You lost me, Mom."

"If Chef Claire decides that she needs some form of change, which I believe she will, the word the three of you should start using is *and*, not *either or*."

"So, you're saying she should open a restaurant down here?"

"Now there's an interesting idea," she said, giving me a sly grin. "This place can always use another great restaurant, especially one run by someone with her skills. Great chefs open new restaurants in different locations all the time, right?"

"Yeah, I imagine they do."

"However, Chef Claire would probably need some working capital to get it off the ground. But between the two of us, that wouldn't be a problem."

"You want us to open another C's down here, don't you?"

"What a great idea, darling," she said, beaming at me. "Now why didn't I think of that?"

"Unbelievable," I said, shaking my head.

"What's the matter, darling?"

"Having us down here on vacation was just part of your plan to get me to move here during the winter, wasn't it?

"Well, I had to start somewhere, didn't I? I couldn't convince you to spend winters here until you'd at least seen the place."

"Geez, Mom," I said, then wanted to kick myself for, once again, sounding like a whiny teenage girl.

"I hate not seeing you for four months of the year, darling."

"I'm supposed to be on vacation."

"And you are. But that doesn't mean you can't do some real thinking while you're down here. Besides, maybe making plans to open a new restaurant will take your mind off that nasty murder."

"You're such a manipulator, Mom," I said, glaring at her.

"That's harsh, darling," she said with a grin. "I much prefer the term *strategist*."

"Tomato, tomahto."

"Of course, the restaurant by itself wouldn't be enough to keep you and Josie busy. So, we'd have to find something to keep the two of you occupied. But I'm sure the two of you can come up with an idea. Perhaps, something along the lines of a four-legged solution."

I stared at her in disbelief and wondered how long she'd been putting her plan together. And despite that fact she was unable to stop meddling in my life, as I glanced outside at the white sand and gentle surf lapping onto the shore, I was forced to admit that it wasn't the craziest idea she'd ever had.

Not that I was about to tell her that.

"I think he was right," I whispered.

"Who was right about what, darling?"

"Gerald. He thinks you're a genius.

"Yes, he does, doesn't he?"

Chapter 14

We removed the top from one of the jeeps and hopped in with me driving. I slowly made my way down the winding driveway and carefully worked my way around the spot where the palm trees had fallen. We waved to the work crew, made our way to the main road, and turned left. Two miles up the road, I turned right, away from the beach, and followed the directions Henry had jotted down for us. I drove in silence and stared out at the road with both hands gripping the steering wheel.

"Okay, Snoopmeister. What's on your mind?"

"I just had one of those conversations with my mother," I said, glancing down at the directions then up at the street signs, several of which were bent at odd angles from the wind.

"Was it one of the *let me give you some friendly advice* chats, or one of the *when I want your opinion, young lady, I'll give it to you?*"

Despite the jumbled collection of thoughts that were weighing on my mind, I laughed and looked over at her.

"Thanks. I needed that."

"So, what did she have to say for herself?"

"She wants us to open another C's down here," I said, turning right.

"Really?" Josie said, frowning.

"Yeah, she says that Chef Claire is getting restless and we should be talking with her using an *additive* approach."

"Yeah, I get that."

"You do? I didn't have a clue what she was talking about at first."

"And you walked yourself right into it, didn't you?" she said, laughing.

"I certainly did. So, what do you think about the idea?"

"Opening a restaurant here, or about Chef Claire starting to think about raising a family?"

"You knew she was thinking about that?"

"Well, it's really not a well-kept secret, Suzy. We're all thinking about it."

"Yeah, I guess we are," I said, glancing down at the directions.

"And your mom figures that would be a way to get you down here four months out of the year," Josie said.

"Yup. She says she misses me."

"I'm sure she does," Josie said, raising her arms above her head to stretch. "We'd need to find some way to stay busy."

"That's what my mom said."

"Well, she's right. Drinking Mudslides on the beach should be a reward at the end of a day's work, not the primary objective."

"Are you sure about that?" I said, grinning at her.

"Pretty sure. But we can spend the rest of the week doing research if you like."

"I'll let you know," I said, coming to a stop in front of a severely damaged property. "This is it."

"Wow. This place got pounded last night."

We hopped out and headed for the verandah. The house was a traditional structure of wood with a tin roof that had come loose in several places. It badly needed a fresh coat of paint, and the picket fence surrounding the property had collapsed on one side. We climbed the short set of steps and knocked loudly on the front door. Moments later, we heard voices coming from the rear of the property, and we walked back down the steps and headed for the backyard. A middle-aged woman and two young children were racing around the yard and doing their best to herd a variety of animals and failing miserably. When the woman saw us, she stopped what she was doing and walked toward us.

"Can I help you?" she said, glancing back and forth at us.

"Hi, I'm Suzy. And this is Josie."

"Nice to meet you. I'm Teresa. Teresa Williams."

"We stopped by about some dogs we found on the beach last night. I think they're strays."

"I see," she said. "What breed?"

"A male bloodhound and a female basset," Josie said. "And their six puppies."

"Yes, I've heard about the adults," she said, nodding. "They've been around for several weeks, but no one has been able to catch them. But I don't imagine anyone has really tried that hard. So, they had a litter?"

"Yes. And they're gorgeous. Is this really an animal shelter?" I said, glancing around at the damage.

"Well, it was," she said, tearing up. "I'm sorry, but I'm afraid the storm has put me out of business."

"Really?" I said.

"Yes, I've been barely hanging on for a while," she said, wiping her eyes with a tissue. "And after the hurricane season ended this year, I decided to roll the dice and cancel my insurance to help my cash flow. I think I just rolled snake eyes."

I watched the two young girls chasing several kittens and a handful of baby ducks. A rooster was strutting his stuff around the yard and occasionally making his presence known with a loud voice.

"You've got quite a menagerie here," Josie said. "Are they your girls?"

"They are. Thankfully, school is out, or I'd be in even worse shape than I am. Girls, one of the piglets is about to head through that gap in the fence. No, over to your right. That's it."

She shook her head and refocused on us.

"I'm really sorry," she said. "But there is no way I'm going to be able to take the dogs in. I'll be lucky if I don't lose half of what I have at the moment."

"Can we help?" I said.

"Aren't you down here on vacation?"

"Yes, we are. We're visiting my mother."

"How nice," she said, smiling. "No, I couldn't impose on you like that."

"It's no trouble," I said.

"And we'd love to help," Josie said. "What can we do?"

"That's so kind of you. Well, if you're any good with a hammer, you could start by seeing if there is something you can do about the fence," she said.

"I noticed your roof took quite a beating," I said.

"Yes," she said, glancing up at it. "I have no idea what I'm going to do about that."

"I think I have an idea," I said, grabbing my phone. "Hey, Mom. Yeah, we found it…No, it's pretty damaged. Is that work crew still there? Great. Would you mind sending them over here as soon as they finish up? Henry has the address…Great. Thanks, Mom."

I put my phone away.

"They'll be here in about an hour," I said.

"What?" she said, staring at me. "Who?"

"There's a work crew at my mom's place. And I asked her to send them over here."

"To fix my roof?"

"Yeah. And anything else that needs to be done," I said.

"But I have no money to pay them," she said, rubbing her head. "Maybe I can work out some sort of payment plan."

"Don't worry about the money," I said. "We'll take care of it."

"Why would you do something that generous for a complete stranger?" she said, giving me a hard stare.

"Well, Teresa," I said, shrugging. "You seem like a lovely woman, and your daughters are gorgeous. But primarily, we're doing it for the animals."

"Absolutely," Josie said, nodding.

"You're animal lovers?"

"Well, we usually spend all our time focused on dogs, but we're basically a soft touch for anything with four legs."

"Then welcome to Grand Cayman," she said, smiling. "We can always use a few more animal lovers around the place."

"I was afraid you were going to say that," I said, laughing.

"You don't think this was part of your mom's plan, do you?" Josie whispered.

"No. It couldn't be, could it?" I said, frowning. "This has to be pure kismet, right?"

"Well, I don't think she controls the weather," Josie said. "But I wouldn't put it past her."

"I'm sorry, but I don't understand," Teresa said.

"Don't worry. You will."

Chapter 15

Southern Spice, a modest looking Indian restaurant not far down the road from my mother's place, didn't have the food-porn look of the high-end restaurants tucked away inside the large resorts on the island, but it smelled fantastic. Whatever the owners had saved on décor, they'd more than made up for in spices, and I perused the menu on an empty stomach with my senses of taste and smell on red alert.

"I always like to order several entrees we can share," my mother said, waving to somebody on the other side of the restaurant.

"That's good," I said. "Because there's no way I'm going to be able to pick just one."

"One?" Josie said, looking up from her menu. "Not a chance. Good call, Mrs. C. I love Indian food."

"Yes, I know, dear," my mother said, glancing around. "I think that the new C's décor should fall somewhere between this and the C's back home. You know, clean and stylish but not showy."

I nodded and gawked at some of the nearby tables to get a good look at some of the dishes.

"So, how was the animal shelter?" my mother said, closing her menu.

"It's in bad shape," I said. "She's been trying to live in the house and also operate the business out of it. And since she doesn't have any working capital, both the house and business have developed slow leaks."

"Which became major floods when that storm rolled through," Josie said.

"Yes, it did look quite rundown when Henry and I drove by the other day," my mother said.

"Henry," I said. "Haven't you learned by now not to humor her?"

Henry laughed and shrugged back at me.

"Hey, she pays me to keep her happy," he said.

"And you do a great job," my mother said, patting his hand. "Did you talk to her about taking the dogs?"

"Mom, if you had seen the condition the place was is, you wouldn't even ask that question."

"That's what I was afraid of. So, the dogs will be occupying my garage for the rest of your visit?"

"I'm sorry, Mom," I said. "But I'm sure you understand."

"Oh, I get it, darling. I just don't like it."

Henry snorted then composed himself when he caught the dirty look my mother was giving him.

"What?" I said.

"It's nothing," Henry said.

"Spill it, Henry," I said.

"I had to go in the garage this afternoon, and your mother was in there playing with the puppies," he said. "Actually, she was rolling around on the floor with them."

"No way," I said, staring at her.

"I wasn't rolling around on the floor," she said. "I was merely making sure they had water."

"We finally wore her down," Josie said. "I knew she was a dog person at heart."

"I most certainly am not. But there's something about the way they look at you with those eyes. It reminds me of the way your father used to look at me."

"With despair and sadness?" I deadpanned.

"Funny, darling. I was referring to love and affection. You're such a pain sometimes."

"You sure you want me around four months out of the year?" I said, laughing.

"Hold that thought," she said, getting up from the table. "I'll be right back."

I watched her head for another table to say hello to a couple who'd just entered the restaurant. A server arrived with a huge tray of appetizers we hadn't ordered.

"Good evening, Henry," the server said. "I've brought your usual appetizer tray. Just let me know if you want anything else. And I'll be back in a bit to take your entrée orders."

"Thanks, Nilesh. It smells fantastic," Henry said, breaking off a piece of hot Naan and dipping it into a bowl of Hummus.

"We're pretty casual down here when we eat, so just help yourself."

"I thought you'd never ask," Josie said, surveying the tray as she developed her plan of attack.

I grabbed a Samosa, savored a bite, then focused on Henry.

"How did you end up working for my mother?" I said.

"We met when I was still working for the local police," Henry said, nodding his approval as he sampled one of the Samosas.

"You were a cop?"

"Twelve years. And then your mother made me an offer I couldn't refuse."

"She can be very persuasive," Josie said, through a mouthful of Chicken Tikka.

"And what exactly is your job?"

Henry shrugged and took a sip of water.

"At first, it was basically just to live in the house and take care of the property when she wasn't on the island. Over the years, my duties have expanded." He glanced at me, realized I wanted a few more details, then continued. "Now, I make sure she's safe and has everything she needs. I do some cooking, I drive her around when necessary, and, in general, provide companionship."

"Companionship? I see," I said, raising an eyebrow that probably came across as accusatory.

"Smooth," Josie said, shaking her head as she reached for a Samosa.

"Are you asking me if I'm sleeping with your mother?"

"Well, actually, I was trying not to come right out and ask the question," I said with a weak smile.

"No, I'm not sleeping with your mother, Suzy. We have more of a brother and sister relationship," he said, tearing off another piece of Naan. "Not that it's any of your business."

"Sorry, Henry. You're right. It's not. But I worry about her."

"As do I," he said. "But as long as I'm around, she's safe and sound."

"Good, I'm glad to hear that," I said, then shifted gears. "So, who do you think killed Wily?"

Henry started at me as he slowly chewed his food. Then he took another sip of water and wiped his mouth.

"Your mother warned me about your...inquisitiveness."

"That's a word for it," Josie said, scanning the appetizer tray.

"I think it's genetic," I said, shrugging. "Blame her."

Henry relaxed and laughed.

"I believe your mother calls it, a dog with a bone," he said. "Perhaps, I was the one who killed him,"

"Interesting," I said, glancing at Josie. "What do you think?"

"Nah," Josie said. "It wasn't Henry."

"You're right. If Wily had been a direct threat to my mom maybe, but I can tell that she wouldn't have gone within a hundred yards of him. Wily was only at dinner because someone else wanted him there."

"Did your mother tell you that?" he said.

"No, she didn't have to," I said.

"Impressive. Do you always think like a cop?"

"Only when I'm forced to be around people instead of dogs. So, do you have any ideas who might have killed him?"

"I have several," he said, sitting back in his chair when the server returned with cold beers for everyone. "Thanks, Nilesh."

"A telepathic waiter," Josie said, taking a sip of beer. "I have to get one of those."

"We come here often," Henry said.

"So, who do you think killed him?" I said.

"Tenacious," he said.

"Henry, she's not going to stop," Josie said. "So, you might as well just tell her."

"Yes, I believe you. My list of suspects has several names on it."

"Seven, right?"

"Actually, yes. How on earth did you know that?"

"Simple math," I said. "There were thirteen people there, not counting the victim. When you eliminate you and my mom, the three of us, and Gerald, you're left with seven people."

"Why have you eliminated Gerald as a suspect?" Henry said.

"Easy. He's the Finance Minister, and he would never do something stupid like killing somebody with that many possible witnesses around. And I think whoever killed Wily did it on impulse driven by emotion. Gerald seems to go through life with his feathers pretty much unruffled. Nothing seems to rattle him."

"That's a very astute observation. I'm impressed."

"Thanks. But even though he wasn't the one who killed him, that's not to say that Gerald wasn't involved."

Henry flinched and stared at me.

"But Gerald would have been involved only if the motive was related to a financial matter. If it was a crime of passion, driven by jealousy, my suspect list looks quite different."

I sat back and took a sip of my beer.

"Is she always like this?" Henry said to Josie.

"This is nothing," Josie said. "You should see her when she's not on vacation."

My mother approached and sat back down at the table.

"What did I miss?"

"Just the usual," Josie said.

"I apologize, Henry," my mother said, laughing. "How hard did she grill you?"

"If the lighting was any brighter, I would have sworn I was back in the police station. But on the other side of the table."

"Darling, must you?" she said, then frowned to herself as she reached for a Samosa. "Look who I'm talking to. Oh, before I forget, the Crenshaws have invited all of us to a barbecue at their place tomorrow night."

"Who are they?" I said, glancing over at the couple's table.

"Just friends, darling. But don't worry, you'll have a great time. Most of the people you spent last night with will all be there, and you have all day tomorrow to come up with your list of questions."

"Now, that's funny," Josie said, raising her glass to my mother in a toast.

"Disagree."

Chapter 16

We spent most of the next day walking the beach and lounging around the pool playing with the dogs. When the sun got too hot for the puppies, we got them settled in the garage then swam and lounged some more as we discussed the possibility and ramifications of relocating here during the winter. By the time we finished that conversation all three of us were worn out, and we headed to our bedrooms to shower and nurse our sunburns. I changed into a pair of shorts and a silk blouse my mother had given me as a Christmas present then headed for the garage. I opened the door and ushered all the dogs outside to take care of their business. Then I got them settled down and headed back inside the house with only a handful of paw prints on my clothes.

"How are they doing?" Josie said as she entered the living room.

"Fed, watered, walked, and settled in."

"Thanks for doing that."

"Yeah, it was a real struggle," I said, laughing. "What are we going to do with them?"

"I have no idea," Josie said.

"Do with who?" Chef Claire said, putting on her earrings as she sat down.

"The dogs," I said.

"I just assumed that we'd take them home with us," she said, shrugging. "How do these look?"

"They look great," Josie said. "Take them home with us. Now, there's an idea."

"Why not?" I said. "I wonder what sort of problem we'd have getting clearance to take them back to the States."

"Let's ask Gerald tonight," Josie said. "He'll either know or know who we need to talk to."

"I'd be worried about putting them on a commercial flight. Especially the puppies."

"Yeah, me too," Josie said.

"I guess we could take a charter flight," I said.

"Expensive," Chef Claire said.

"Leave that to me. Somebody owes me a favor."

"I've been thinking about the idea of opening another restaurant," Chef Claire said.

"I thought we agreed we weren't going to think about it the rest of the day," Josie said.

"I do some of my best thinking in the shower," Chef Claire said.

"That's odd. I would have thought you'd be doing all your thinking in there about a certain detective," Josie deadpanned.

"Shut it."

"Oh, I hit a nerve," Josie said. "Do tell."

Chef Claire made a face at her, then draped one leg over the other.

"He's really nice. And cute as all get out," she said. "But he comes across as a bit desperate."

"My mother said he really wants to settle down and raise a family."

"Is there anything your mother doesn't know?" Chef Claire said, shaking her head.

"Well, there was one time in high school when I slipped out of the house at night I don't think she ever figured out."

"I knew all about it, darling. But since I liked Jimmy, I decided not to make a big deal of it. I know how easily you get embarrassed."

Startled, I turned around and saw my mother standing right behind me.

"Does that answer your question?" I said to Chef Claire.

My mother beamed at me, then glanced around.

"What are we talking about?" she said.

"The dogs. Since there's no place to take them, and we don't have enough time to find them good homes, we're thinking about taking them back to the Inn with us," I said. "But we're nervous about them flying commercial."

"Okay," she said, nodding.

"We thought we'd catch a charter flight home," I said. "And I thought it would be very generous of you to pick up the tab."

"Did you now?" my mother said, giving me a small smile.

"Yes. It would be a nice way to thank us for agreeing to your nefarious plan," I said.

"I see. Nefarious, huh? And if I say no?"

"Well, then I guess we could always leave all eight of them here with you," I deadpanned.

She stared at me, then nodded.

"Okay, darling. Well played. I'll see what I can do. Are we ready to go? I thought we'd take both jeeps. No sense being crammed into one," she said, tossing a set of keys to me. "Just follow Henry and I. Come on. Chop, chop."

Chapter 17

As we followed Henry on the drive to the barbecue, we noticed remnants from the storm all over the beach and along the side of the road. But when we pulled into the Crenshaw's driveway, an immaculate landscape greeted us. Either the storm had spared the large property, which seemed highly unlikely, or they had also commandeered a work crew to clean up and get the place back to what could only be called pristine condition. By comparison, the house made my mother's place look like a condo, and I parked and stared at the house dumbfounded.

"Well, if I ever come into big money," Chef Claire said, hopping out of the jeep. "The Caymans are definitely the place I'm going to try to hide it."

"No kidding," Josie said. "I've seen smaller hotels. Did your mom say what these people do for a living?"

"Apparently, he's in finance," I said. "And she drinks."

"Ah, the mysterious finance," Josie said.

My mother waved for us to follow her and Henry as they headed around the outside of the house toward the beach.

"It's not too late," I said, feeling intimidated by our surroundings. "We can still make our escape and head out for Mudslides and a burger."

"Aren't you curious to see what it looks like inside?" Chef Claire said.

"Maybe a bit. What the heck, since we're already here," I said, then glanced at Josie. "You ready for this?"

"Sure, why not?" she said. "Do you feel like walking, or should we call a cab?"

We followed the path my mother had taken then found ourselves looking out on another magnificent stretch of sand. All three of us turned around and craned our necks up at the multi-level house.

"I sure hope their cleaning lady does windows," Josie said, laughing. "Geez, that's a lot of glass."

"There you are," my mother said as she approached. "What do you think of the place?"

"We were just wondering if we can get a drink now or if we should wait until after we check in," I said, still taking in the massive home.

"Yes," my mother said, glancing around the house. "It does have kind of a Ritz Carlton feel to it, doesn't it?"

"Mom, who are these people?" I said.

"Just a couple of business acquaintances, darling. Come on, let me introduce you."

We followed her across the lawn to where a gray-haired man in his sixties was holding court. The small audience was hanging on every word, nodding and laughing as they sipped their cocktails. A woman in her thirties had her arm draped over the man's shoulder, and I couldn't tell if it was an expression of affection or if it was the only thing keeping her upright.

"And then I said, that's okay, I'll just move it all to the Bahamas. I'm sure they'll be more than happy to take it."

Nod. Laugh. Sip.

"You should have seen the look on his face."

Nod. Laugh. Sip.

"It was beautiful."

Nod. Laugh. Sip.

Then he caught a glimpse of my mother out of the corner of his eye, and he turned toward her. The woman hanging onto his shoulder lost her grip, stumbled, then dropped to one knee on the grass. Unfazed, she picked herself up and wobbled for a second. Then she looked down at the glass in her hand and smiled when she realized she hadn't spilled a drop.

"Hi, Jerome," my mother said. "Thanks so much for inviting us."

"We're so glad you could make it," he said.

"So glad," the woman said, raising her glass to my mother.

"I'd like you to meet my daughter Suzy and her business partners, Josie and Chef Claire. Ladies, this is Jerome and Gloria Crenshaw."

We murmured hellos and did our best not to stare at the woman with the unfixed gaze.

"It's very nice to meet you," he said, sizing all three of us up.

"Very nice," the woman slurred.

"Gloria, why don't you see if you can get both of us a refill?" Jerome said, giving his wife what looked like a very sad smile. "And send one of the servers over here to take drink orders for our new arrivals."

"You got it," she said, staggering off toward one of the temporary bars that had been set up on the lawn.

"Don't mind her," Jerome said. "She just got a bit of an early start."

"My guess is sometime in July," Josie whispered.

"Don't start," I whispered back, then focused on Jerome. "You have a magnificent home."

"Thank you very much," he said, nodding. "It's way too much house for two people, but at thirty million, it was just too much of a bargain to pass up."

"Sure, sure."

"If you'll excuse me, I believe I hear Gloria making a bit of a ruckus over there. I should probably go check it out."

"Of course," my mother said. "We'll see you later. And thanks again for the invitation, Jerome."

He waved without looking back and strode across the lawn toward the commotion.

"A *bargain*? At *thirty million*?" Josie said.

"Yeah, I almost fell over when he said that," Chef Claire said.

"They live in a different world from the rest of us," my mother said. "But in the end, they're just human beings like the rest of us."

"I guess," Josie said, frowning. "They seem human enough."

Chef Claire and I snorted, then cut it short when we caught the look my mother was giving us.

"It's like the old saying goes," my mother said. "They put their pants on one leg at a time, just like everyone else."

"Or in Gloria's case," I said, nodding off into the distance. "Take them off one leg at a time."

Jerome was chasing his naked wife down the beach toward the water's edge. Apparently, Gloria had decided a swim before dinner sounded good. Jerome ended up tackling her in the sand, and he held her down until one of the servers arrived with a blanket. Jerome wrapped the blanket around her, then carried her back toward the house kicking and screaming. Halfway there, she nodded off for a nap. Jerome, trailed by two women I assumed were housekeepers, carried his wife inside, and they all disappeared from view. A few minutes later, Jerome emerged and headed for the barbecue area, red-faced.

"What is he doing with that woman, Mom?"

"It's her money, darling."

"What?"

"Family money. Big family money. And she inherited all of it."

"Then let me rephrase the question," I said. "What on earth is she doing with him? He has to be thirty years older than she is."

"Good question, darling. And it's one a lot of us ask all the time."

Chapter 18

The food was remarkable. Chef Claire and I forced ourselves to stop at two helpings, but Josie went back for a third. When we laughingly called her a little piggy, she turned indignant and insisted that since her third serving had been small, technically, she'd only had two and a half. We eventually conceded the point just to get her to shut up, and we sat quietly staring out at the ocean while we digested our dinner.

After we had eaten, my mother got up and headed for Gerald who was sitting off by himself. She stretched out in the lounge chair next to his, and they began an animated conversation. I watched them for a few minutes until Bill and Jerry from Buffalo sat down at our table.

"Did you get a chance to swim with the stingrays yet?" Bill said.

"We've been a bit busy with the dogs since the storm," I said. "Maybe tomorrow."

"Oh, you have to do it. It's a must," Jerry said.

"It's definitely on our list," I said, agreeing just to get off the subject. There was a better chance I'd adopt a fish-based diet than swim with a bunch of sea creatures that could kill me with a flick of their tail. "This is quite a collection of people."

Bill and Jerry glanced around and nodded.

"Yeah, I guess," Bill said. "Most of them have more money than brains."

"But they're nice enough. And the Crenshaw's parties are legendary."

Bill snorted and glanced around at the crowd.

"What do you guys do down here?" I said.

"Us?" Bill said. "Not a heck of a lot. We spend a lot of time at the beach. We like to eat and drink."

"And we spend a lot of time in bed," Jerry said.

"Yes, we do, don't we?" Bill said, grinning at his wife then glancing over at me. "You know how that goes."

"Sure, sure," I said. "But I was talking about what you do for work."

"Work?" Bill grunted with a scowl. "I'm done with that. The closest we get to work these days is when we play with our money."

"That sounds more like exercise," I said.

"You really are too funny," Jerry said.

"Yeah, I know. Just like my mother."

"Exactly," Bill said.

"What do you know about him?" I said, nodding at the landscape artist who was standing nearby talking with Prunella.

"Sky?" Bill said, shrugging. "He's okay. A little artsy for my taste, but I have to give him credit. He's making a small fortune selling his paintings to tourists from the cruise ships."

"I hear he likes to do another type of painting. More of a…portrait style."

Jerry flushed a color of red usually reserved for sunburned tourists.

"Uh, yeah," Bill said. "I've heard that rumor, too."

"It's probably a nice change from the landscapes," I said, wondering if Jerry had actually posed for the artist, or had merely been asked. "How do you know the Crenshaws?"

"We all know each other down here," Bill said, suddenly not as chatty. "At least all the people with a few nickels to rub together."

"That makes sense. It's a small island, right?"

"Yes, it certainly is," Jerry said, glancing at her husband.

Bill and Jerry got up from the table and excused themselves then headed for the beach. I watched them slowly stroll along the edge of the water until they disappeared into the darkness. I looked around the crowd and spotted Jerome who seemed to have recovered from his earlier battle on the beach with his wife. He was chatting with Thomas and Sally, the banker and his wife I'd met the other night at my mom's house. Sally kept glancing over at Sky and Prunella and shooting daggers at the artist. Prunella, who had a hand up the inside of Sky's shirt, seemed to be doing a good job shaking off her husband's death. I looked around to see if I could spot Gloria in the crowd, but couldn't find her. Still sleeping it off, I decided.

Then a server carrying a tray with an envelope sitting on it approached Jerome Crenshaw. He seemed confused at first, then took the envelope and waited for the server to depart. He opened the envelope, read the note inside, then frowned and scanned the crowd. Apparently not finding the person he was looking for, he slipped the note into his shirt pocket then headed inside the house. I resumed studying the crowd that was still loud with laughter but seemed to be getting smaller by the minute. I checked my watch and frowned.

"What's the matter?" Josie said. "You've got that look."

"Where the heck is everybody?" I said. "It's barely nine o'clock."

"They've been slipping away in pairs," Chef Claire said.

"Really?" I said, glancing around.

"And I've seen a lot of mixed pairs," Chef Claire said. "If you catch my drift."

"Non-spousal hook ups?" Josie said.

"Exactly," Chef Claire said.

"Do you think this is some sort of swingers group?" I said, frowning.

"I don't know what it is," Chef Claire said. "But there are a lot of strange people here. And I'm getting a very weird vibe."

"Me too," Josie said. "When I was at the bar earlier, some guy asked me if I was having a good time, said something about it being a good night to make a memory, and then tried to use some sort of secret handshake with me."

"You're kidding, right?" I said.

"I wish. At first, I thought he was just hammered. Then I saw him pull the same stunt with someone else. They headed inside the house and haven't been back since."

"What the heck is my mother doing here?" I said.

Chef Claire and Josie both stared at me until the lightbulb went off.

"My mom? A swinger? Not a chance."

"Stranger things have happened," Josie said.

"Maybe in the Twilight Zone," I said, shaking my head. "My mom? No way."

"Yeah, I'm sure you're right," Josie said, not sounding sure about it at all.

Then the night air was pierced with the sound of a man's wail. The cry seemed to last forever and reminded me of a singer holding the last note of a song. But the wail was by no means melodic, just filled with despair and a touch of terror. Everyone in the crowd turned to stare at the house, and I noticed several pairs of eyes popping up from various places around the lawn. Moments later, Jerome Crenshaw slowly stepped through the front door into the light. He stood rigidly, obviously in shock, and his hands and the front of his shirt were covered in blood.

"Is he hurt, or is that someone else's blood?" Chef Claire said, squinting at the house.

Crenshaw dropped to his knees clutching his chest, then fell forward on the verandah.

"I'm gonna go with his," Josie said, standing up to get a better look. "Should we do something?"

"Like what?" I said.

"I don't know," she said. "Maybe call an ambulance."

"How many doctors have you met here tonight?" I said.

"Probably half a dozen. Yeah, good point. I'm sure they'll know what to do. Then maybe we should call the cops."

"The National Commissioner of Police is here," Chef Claire said. "I met him earlier, but I think I saw him head for the beach with one of the doctor's wives."

"Geez, if we had wanted weirdness and murder, we could have just stayed home," Josie said.

"I was just thinking the same thing," I said, still staring at the house. "Here comes somebody. It's Gerald."

We watched Gerald kneel down and gently roll the body over. He checked Jerome's pulse, then slowly shook his head. He remained bent down and started talking over his shoulder to two other men who had arrived. Soon, there were several other people staring over Gerald's head whispering nervously to each other. But I didn't watch their conversation. I was focused on the body, and when I caught a glimpse of the reflected light, I exhaled audibly and shook my head.

"Is that what I think it is?" I said.

"Yeah, I think it is," Josie said.

"I don't see anything," Chef Claire said.

"The right side of his chest," Josie said.

Chef Claire focused hard then gasped. "I don't believe it." She glanced back and forth at us. "Really?"

"Yup. Skewer," Josie said. "No vegetables."

"Coincidence?" Chef Claire said.

"Doubtful," I said.

"Agree," Josie said. "Okay, I'll be right back."

"Where are you going?" I said.

"To the grill, before they shut it down," she said. "I have a feeling we're going to be here for a while."

I glanced at Chef Claire, and she nodded.

"Good call," I said, hustling to catch up.

Chapter 19

Josie was right. We were there awhile. Three and a half hours to be exact. We snacked on a wide assortment from the grill and talked in soft voices with Henry and my mother while we waited for our turn to speak with the police. When the cops ran out of questions or got tired of asking the same ones over and over, and finally let everyone leave, no one had been arrested. We drove back to my mom's place in silence and decided to sit around the pool with the dogs.

I looked over at my mother who was stretched out on a lounge chair with her eyes closed and one of the puppies sleeping on her chest. Knowing all too well that I was on the prowl, she continued to avoid me, and my list of questions for her continued to grow. Unwilling to wait any longer, I stretched out on the adjacent lounge chair and waited for her to acknowledge my presence. When the puppy woke up and stared at me, my mother was unable to maintain her charade any longer, and she turned her head and gave me her best laconic look.

"Is something on your mind, darling?"

"Where do I begin?"

"Is that rhetorical, or are you really not sure?"

"Don't start, Mom."

"Why don't you just jump in? I'm sure you'll eventually find your footing," she said, closing her eyes as the puppy settled back down on her chest.

"How could you do that, Mom?"

"Do what?"

"Take us to a swinger's party."

She opened her eyes and looked at me. "A man gets stabbed in the chest inside his own house, and that's what you're worried about?"

I'd been expecting a fastball, but I whiffed completely on the slow curve she'd thrown.

"You're deflecting," I said, "And completely avoiding my question."

"Okay, darling, I'll play," she said, sitting up on the lounge chair. "Before I agreed to go to the Crenshaw's barbecue, I specifically asked them when I saw them at the restaurant if the party was going to be one of what they call, a Memory Maker."

"Josie mentioned that someone used that exact phrase on her," I said.

"Only one?"

"What?"

"I can't believe that only one person approached her," my mother said.

"Well, you know how people tend to keep their distance when she has silverware in her hands."

"Sure, sure," she said, nodding. "How about you, darling? How many proposals did you get?"

"What?"

"I'm just curious."

"Thankfully, I didn't get any, Mom."

"You must have been hiding in the shadows all night. You really need to get out there more. As I was saying, I asked the Crenshaws at the restaurant, and they assured me that it wasn't one of those parties."

"So, you're saying they lied to you?"

"Not at all," she said, rubbing the puppy's head with both hands. "This little guy really is cute, isn't he?"

"They're all cute, Mom," I said, shaking my head. "They're puppies. So, what happened that caused an orgy to break out?"

"That wasn't an orgy, darling," she said. "Trust me, you'd have noticed if it were."

"Mom! Enough."

"Relax, darling. I'm just having a little fun with you. You're supposed to be on vacation, remember?"

"Oh, I'm so sorry. I completely forgot. The two murders and a beach sex party must be clouding my thinking."

"Don't do drama queen, darling. It's not your strong suit." She held up the puppy and gently rocked him back and forth in the air. "Yes, she's being very dramatic, isn't she?"

"What happened at the barbecue, Mom?"

116

"You mean apart from the host getting stabbed to death, right?"

I took several deep breaths to calm myself and scratched at my sunburn.

"Yes, Mom," I said, eventually. "Apart from that."

"If you'll excuse the rather obvious pun, my guess is that the guests just took things into their own hands. I'm sure that many of them are regulars at the Memory Maker events and didn't make the distinction."

"I can believe you participate in something like that."

"Is that what you think?" she said, dumbfounded. "That's the reason for your hissy fit?"

"It's not a hissy fit."

"Darling, I assure you that I do not participate in those events. And I'm surprised and hurt that you would even think that."

"Yeah, you look absolutely crushed, Mom," I said, glaring back at her.

"Much better, darling. That's the spirit I like to see. I only agreed to attend last night after I was specifically told it wasn't that kind of party. I wouldn't subject you and the girls to that."

"But you've been to those parties in the past, right?"

"Just after your father died, I was invited to one. And I went, saw what was going on, then left immediately."

"Really?"

"Darling, I know how your mind tends to…drift from time to time. And while you might consider me somewhat prolific when it comes to the men in my life, I assure you that I'm a traditionalist to the core."

"But if you know what those people are like, why do you continue to hang out with them?"

"One doesn't always get to pick and choose when it comes to business, darling," she said, sighing as the puppy tucked himself under her arm. "He really is adorable."

"Can I ask you what sort of business you're referring to?"

"Oh, I wish you wouldn't, darling," she said, shaking her head.

"Because you don't want to have to lie to me?"

"No. Because it's none of your business."

I'd got caught looking at the fastball right down the middle, and I acknowledged my whiff with miffed silence. I'd come into this conversation convinced I had the upper hand and moral authority on my side. Now, I was wondering if I'd be able to get out unscathed. She glanced over and gave me a coy smile that, if she hadn't been my mother, I might have tried to knock off her face.

"Since both of them were killed in the same way, do you think the same person committed them?"

"Oh, a tactical retreat to a new topic. Good call, darling."

"You really need to learn how to win gracefully, Mom."

"And you need to stop believing that I would ever allow myself to be passed back and forth between different men like a piece of meat," she said, giving me her best *how dare you* look.

"I'm sorry, Mom," I said, conceding defeat. "How about we just start over?"

"That sounds like a great idea. So, tell me, did you and the girls have a nice time tonight?"

Another slow curve that I flinched at before it sailed by and caught the outside corner. Since I'd completely whiffed without even getting the bat off my shoulder, I decided to slink back to the dugout.

"Nice of you to just let it go, Mom," I said, exhaling loudly as I climbed out of the lounge chair.

"You started it, darling."

Chapter 20

Deciding that we were too tired for sightseeing, and finding the idea of swimming with a group of hungry stingrays too bizarre to even consider, we opted for another day of lounging by the pool playing with the puppies and seeing how well they handled the water. The bloodhound loved it, and we couldn't have gotten him out of the pool if we'd wanted to. But the basset, as was often the case with the breed, wasn't a great swimmer. And while she could work her way in and out of the water without drowning, it was obvious it wasn't her favorite thing to do. She spent most of the morning under Chef Claire's lounge chair in the shade keeping a close eye on the puppies who were frolicking in the shallow end of the pool with the three of us. Eventually, they wore themselves out, and they joined their mama under the lounge chair for an extended nap. Even the bloodhound got tired, and he climbed out of the pool, paused to shake water all over me, and trotted over to join Josie on her lounge chair. Josie made room for him and rubbed his head as she glanced around the property.

"I could get used to this," she said, taking a sip of juice.

"I think I'm already there," Chef Claire said. "By the way, the detective asked me out again."

"When?" I said.

"Last night. He slipped the question in right after he asked me where I was when Crenshaw got stabbed."

"What did you tell him?" Josie said.

"That I was sitting at the table with the two of you the whole time," Chef Claire deadpanned.

"Funny," Josie said.

"I told him I was busy."

"Because he comes across as way too desperate?" I said.

"Yeah. I'm not good with desperate."

"Me either," I said.

"Really? I would have thought desperate was right up your alley," Josie said, glancing over and grinning.

"Shut it," I said, tossing aside the magazine I'd spent all of ten minutes reading cover to cover. "What's your take on Crenshaw getting killed the same way as Wily?"

"Well, if I spent any time thinking about it, which I'm desperately trying to avoid doing, at first glance, it would appear that the same person committed both murders," Josie said.

"Yes, it does," I said, nodding.

"Which is why you *don't* think it was the same person, right?"

"You know me so well."

"How did you know she was thinking that?" Chef Claire said to Josie.

"Because Suzy is always drawn to counterintuitive solutions," Josie said.

"Well done," I said. "You have been paying attention."

"And the smell of burning neurons is particularly strong this morning," she said.

"It's just too obvious. And by killing Crenshaw that way, it's going to focus all the police attention on the people who were here at the house when Wily got killed. That's the perfect way for Crenshaw's killer to deflect all the attention."

"Maybe it's a serial killer," Chef Claire said, frowning. "Don't they usually follow the same pattern?"

"The Grillmeister Killer," Josie said, laughing. "Maybe we should be on the lookout for a chef who secretly longs to be a bullfighter."

"What on earth are you talking about?" I said, staring at her.

"Grilling…piercing swords…never mind," she said, shaking her head. "I thought it was clever."

"Well, don't look at me," Chef Claire said. "I haven't been near a kitchen all week."

"I think the motive has to be related to money," I said.

"So, you've moved away from your jealousy theory?" Josie said, grudgingly giving more room to the bloodhound. "Well, excuse me. Am I getting in the way of your beauty sleep?"

"We really need to give him a name, so he'll know when you're talking to him," I said.

"Yeah. I think we should call him Bailey," Josie said.

"As in Bailey's Irish Cream?" Chef Claire said.

"Exactly. It seems appropriate, doesn't it?"

"Well, it's probably better than calling him Mudslide," I said. "I just don't think jealousy is the motive."

"Why not?" Josie said, giving up and moving to a new lounge chair.

"Because everybody seems to be sleeping with each other. What on earth would anyone have to be jealous about?"

"I'm sure those people would be able to come up with a reason," Chef Claire said. "I don't care if it does looks like a Ritz Carlton, if we move down here, that place is off limits."

Josie and I glanced at each other and nodded.

"Agreed."

"I was thinking about asking around to see if there are any big financial deals in the works at the moment," I said.

"Suzy, it's the Cayman Islands," Josie said, laughing. "There's always a big deal in the works."

"Yeah, you're probably right. But maybe tomorrow we can head into town and do a little snooping."

"I thought we decided to charter a boat and go snorkeling," Josie said.

"That's right," I said. "Snorkeling does sound good."

"And you mentioned doing a bit of fishing while we're out there," Chef Claire said.

"I would love to go fishing," I said, nodding.

"Good. Then it's all settled," Josie said. "We're going to spend tomorrow on the water."

"Yes," I said. "Now, all we need to do is figure out who else to invite."

Josie glanced at Chef Claire, then shook her head at me.

"Unbelievable."

Chapter 21

I leaned against a dock piling and nudged Chef Claire with an elbow. We glanced down the dock and watched Josie struggle with the weight of the ice chest she was lugging with both hands. She saw us, set the chest down on the dock and waited. We both gave her a small wave and stayed right where we were.

"We should probably give her a hand," Chef Claire said.

"Absolutely not," I said, laughing. "I told her if she decided to buy all that food, she was going to have to carry it by herself."

Josie resumed her wobbly trek down the dock, glaring at us the entire time. When she arrived, she set the chest down with a thud and ignored us as she stared out at the ocean.

"Did you remember to bring the side of beef?" I said, rummaging through the packed chest.

"Shut it. And thanks for the help."

"Let me give you a hand with that," the captain said as he hopped off the charter boat onto the dock.

Captain Jack, as he insisted on being called, was somewhere in his late forties with sun-bleached hair and a deep tan. He was whistling a jaunty sea tune that really didn't have a melody, and he had a bounce to his step intended to let everyone know he didn't have a care in the world. He casually reached down to lift the ice chest, grunted loudly, then staggered a few steps forward before setting it back down on the dock. Captain Jack grimaced and grabbed his lower back.

"What the heck have you got in there? A dead body?" he said, frowning.

"Oh, let's hope not," I said.

"You do know this is what's called a *day* trip, right?" the captain said. "As in one."

"You'll all be thanking me later," Josie said.

He bent down and used his legs to lift it. Carrying the ice chest in his arms, he eventually managed to get it onto the boat without falling in. I looked down the dock and saw my mother and Henry, trailed closely by Bill and Jerry from Buffalo heading toward us. Behind them, Sky and Sally were slowly strolling up the dock and doing everything they could to keep their hands off each other.

"Well, it's not swimming with the stingrays," Bill said, glancing up at the boat. "But it ain't bad. It ain't bad at all."

"Thanks so much for inviting us along," Jerry said. "A day of diving sounds perfect. We're very excited."

"Glad you could make it. It should be a fun day. Hi, Henry."

"Hi, Suzy," he said, giving me a puzzled look. "You're going diving, huh?"

"Yes. And maybe we'll do a little fishing."

"It looks like a nice day for a little snoop-fishing. I'd be shocked if you didn't take advantage of it," my mother said, giving me a quick hug.

"Thanks for coming."

"I hope you know what you're doing," my mother whispered into my ear.

"Me too, Mom," I said as I waved to Sky and Sally.

"If you embarrass me, I swear I'm going to make you pay," she whispered as she released me and gave the approaching couple a friendly wave.

"I have no doubt about it, Mom," I said, then took a few steps toward Sky and Sally and shaking hands with both of them. "I'm so glad you could make it."

"I appreciate the offer," Sally said. "A day on the water sounds fantastic. And Thomas sends his regrets. He simply couldn't get away from the office today."

"That's too bad. Hey, Sky. What's that?"

"It's my sketchpad," he said, holding it up for me to see. "You never know when it might come in handy."

"Well, would you look at that, Josie?" I said, half-turning to beam at her. "Sky brought his sketchpad."

"Good for Sky," she mumbled, climbing aboard.

Everyone followed her, and we were soon sitting around a padded U-shaped seat that ran across the stern and halfway up both sides. I put my sunglasses on, pulled my hat lower, and transitioned into full-on snoop mode. But other than deciding that Sky and Sally were trying to figure out a spot where they could be alone and that Josie was hungry, everything else remained a mystery since the boat ride was short. I'd barely gotten my neurons firing before Captain Jack slowed the boat, then anchored and climbed down from the captain's chair to the deck. He glanced around at us with a huge smile, which must have been very easy for him since he spent his life taking people out on his boat. He looked out at the ocean and started his spiel.

"Okay, the first thing I need to do is to get a count on how many of you are going to be diving the reefs. I'd hate to lose any of you. The Tourism Bureau would never forgive me," Captain Jack said, chuckling at the joke I was sure he told every day.

Josie and I raised our hands along with Bill and Jerry.

"Okay, the four of you. And I will need to see your certification cards," he said, then glanced at Bill and Jerry. "I see you two have brought your own gear."

"Yes," Jerry said. "Eventually, it just made more sense for us to buy our own."

"Exactly," Bill said, nodding. "Good financial sense."

Captain Jack gave them a weak smile. If he gave a hoot about the couple's good financial sense, it certainly didn't show.

"Okay, the rest of you will be snorkeling," Captain Jack said, jotting down a note. "Four divers, five snorkelers. "The snorkeling gear is in the bin right over there. Help yourself. You'll have plenty to see around both reefs, so please don't wander off too far." Then he looked at us. "Let's get some diving gear for you two. Follow me."

We followed him to the bow where he already had several tanks and regulators laid out next to masks and fins.

"These are ninety-minute tanks," he said, holding one up. "But I always ask folks not to cut it too close. So, if you wouldn't mind surfacing after seventy-five minutes, I'd appreciate it. If you want to keep diving after that, we'll just get you a fresh tank of air. Got it? I assume at least one of you is wearing a waterproof watch."

"Got it," we said in unison and held up our arms for him to see our watches.

"Perfect. Let's see," he said, glancing around. "What else? Oh, yeah. I have wetsuits if you want, but most people don't bother since the water is so warm."

"We don't want suits, right?" I said, glancing at Josie who also seemed to find the idea ridiculous.

"No wetsuits," he said, nodding. "Good call. Let's get these tanks on so I can check to make sure you actually know what you're doing."

We pulled the tanks on, tested the regulators, and Captain Jack nodded his approval. We removed the tanks, grabbed masks and fins then followed him back to the group. The snorkelers were ready to go, and when I caught a glimpse of Sky in a lime green Speedo, I almost lost it. Josie flinched as well, then smiled when she saw the look on my mother's face. Chef Claire was staring out at the ocean, and I thought I saw a bit of blood on her lower lip. Captain Jack, obviously used to seeing all sorts of things from both tourists and locals alike, shook his head as if to clear it, then pointed out at the ocean.

"Let's hope the sharks aren't attracted to lime green," he whispered. "Okay, folks, you've got a beautiful day here. Most of the cruise ships have departed, and I'm not expecting to see the next batch until later tonight or tomorrow. As such, it should be relatively quiet out there. But that doesn't mean all of you can drop your guard and do something stupid." He looked over at Bill and Jerry. "You're locals, so I assume you've been here before?"

"Many times," Jerry said.

"Thirteen," Bill said, nodding.

"Okay, lucky thirteen," he said, nodding. "But Suzy and Josie have never been here before so do the right thing and keep an eye on them, okay?"

"Of course," Bill said.

"Thank you," my mother said.

"For those of you who haven't been here before, let me spend just a couple of minutes explaining what we're looking at. To your left is what's called Devil's Grotto. And over there to your right is Eden Rock. In my opinion, they are two of the world's best shallow reefs for snorkeling and diving. When you get in the water, you'll soon see the coral reefs, and they'll only be a few feet below the surface. Then you're going to see the bottom begin to slope away, and you'll discover a forty-foot vertical drop."

"Forty feet? I don't think I can hold my breath that long," Sky said.

"I was talking to the divers," Captain Jack said to Sky without actually looking at him.

130

"Oh. Sorry."

"Both Eden Rock and Devil's Grotto are filled with tunnels and caves you'll have a great time exploring. And while you shouldn't have to worry about getting turned around down there, if you do, just remember to look up. I'm going to string a yellow buoy off the boat with a long, bright yellow cord attached to it. Between that and the bottom of the boat, you have no reason in the world to get lost. Am I making myself clear?"

"Yes, Dad," Josie deadpanned.

Captain Jack laughed, but then turned serious again. "I'm not kidding. Safety first. Nothing ruins a vacation faster than an accidental drowning."

"Or a skewer in the chest," Josie whispered.

"What?" Captain Jack said, frowning.

"Nothing. Safety first. Message received loud and clear, Captain." She gave him a snappy salute and grinned at him.

"Is she always like this?" Captain Jack said to me.

"This is nothing."

"Okay, then. The day's wasting away. Let's get rolling."

I stripped down to my two-piece swimsuit and hoisted the air tank over my back. I got an admiring once-over from Sky that made me uncomfortable. But when Josie removed her shorts and tee shirt, Sky seemed to stagger like he'd been hit and made a sound that was a cross between a gasp and a groan. Sally let it go for a couple seconds, then squeezed his hand hard.

"Definitely a good call on the wetsuits," Captain Jack whispered as he did his best not to stare.

"What?" Josie said, fiddling with her regulator.

"Nothing."

The snorkelers went first, and we watched them glide their way from the boat as we secured our tanks and checked the air flow one more time. Bill and Jerry both flopped backward over the boat like a couple of pros. Josie and I opted to ease our way into the water. After a few seconds in the water, my training came back to me, and I followed Josie toward Devil's Grotto, past the coral reef then down to deeper water.

Soon, we had our choice of caverns to explore, and Josie pointed at a stream of light that seemed to be coming from an opening in the ocean floor. But I knew that it was actually the other way around, and the light was coming from the sun that seemed to be boring into the water. Josie waited until she got Bill and Jerry's attention, and the four of us headed down inside a cavern that was a combination of white light, bright blue, and not far from the edge of the light, jet black. The scene was both beautiful and a bit spooky at the same time, and we reached the ocean floor and glanced around. It was thumbs-up all around, then Bill pointed at something. I followed his hand and stared in wonder at thousands of tiny fish swirling in the light that provided a dazzling silvery shine. Then the fish disappeared, and the silvery shine was replaced by a large shadow. Having what I considered to be a healthy respect, combined with intense fear, for sharks, I worked my way back to the edge of the cavern and was surrounded by the dark. Trying to control my breathing, I waited for whatever was producing the shadow to appear, then relaxed and stared open-mouthed as a large tarpon glided through the cavern then disappeared through an opening in a flash.

Josie glanced over and mouthed *Wow* through her mask. I nodded and looked around for Bill and Jerry who were nowhere to be seen. Since they were experienced divers, I didn't give it two thoughts and Josie and I swam to the other side of the cavern, then spotted another stream of light and followed it.

We spent the next forty-five minutes mesmerized by the underwater world, then exited one of the caverns through another beam of light and gently kicked our fins as we slowly rose. Josie and I broke the surface and waved to Bill and Jerry who were treading water a few feet away.

"I finally feel like we're actually on vacation," I said.

"Me too. That was fantastic," Josie said, removing her mask.

"Incredible," I said. "We're going to have to do this again."

"Great, huh?" Jerry said as she swam closer.

"The best," I said, nodding.

"Now you know why we love it so much," Bill said. "It truly is a paradise down here."

Then we heard a woman scream, and I glanced around panicked as I searched for signs of my mother. But she and Henry were off snorkeling by themselves and obviously quite safe. Then

I saw Sally waving her arms frantically about a hundred feet to our right.

"What's the matter?" I called.

"It's Sky," she called at the top of her lungs. "I think he went under. I don't see him anywhere."

"What?" Bill said, immediately going under the water and heading toward the frantic woman.

We followed and submerged, kicking our legs as fast as we could. When we saw Sally's legs above us, we dove straight down. We were on the outer edge of the coral reef, and I spotted something lime green amid a patch of red and purple coral about ten feet below the surface. Sky was still kicking his legs and struggling to free himself, but it was obvious he was quickly running out of air. His body was horizontal in the water, and I noticed a piece of metal that appeared to be stuck on the reef. On closer inspection, I couldn't miss the fact that the same piece of metal was sticking out of Sky's shoulder.

All four of us arrived around the same time, and Josie took a big gulp of air, then inserted the respirator into Sky's mouth. He sucked on it hard, then blew a massive string of bubbles that floated toward the surface. Josie gave him another hit of air, then continued to share it with him while the rest of us did our best to pull the piece of metal from the reef. When we eventually got Sky free, Jerry and Bill gently held him as they headed back up to the surface.

When Josie and I surfaced, we looked at Sky who was gasping for air and groaning in pain. I recognized the object sticking out of his shoulder and grimaced. Josie shook her head in disbelief.

"He got shot by a spear gun?" she said. "What the heck is going on?

"Maybe somebody was fishing and mistook him for a fish," I said, frowning at how strange it sounded even as the words were coming out of my mouth.

"In that Speedo?" she said. "Highly unlikely."

"Well, if it wasn't an accident," I said, staring at the bleeding Sky. "I guess that can only mean one thing."

"I can't wait to hear this."

"Maybe the skewer killer has gone high-tech."

"Now there's a cheery thought. Let's help Bill and Jerry get him back to the boat," Josie said. "He's bleeding pretty bad, and *that* can only mean one thing."

"Sharks," I whispered as I frantically scanned the surface of the water for fins.

"Nothing gets past you."

Chapter 22

When we got Sky back to the boat, Captain Jack was staring down at us in the water and glaring at Sky. Given the lime-green Speedo, I could understand a bit of good natured ribbing, perhaps even ridicule, but Captain Jack seemed furious. Since the guy had been shot in the shoulder by a spear gun, I thought his reaction was a bit over the top. But Captain Jack, way past simple criticism, was bordering on open hostility.

"What on earth is the matter with you?" Captain Jack yelled as he glared down at the artist.

"I got shot in the shoulder," Sky said weakly as he stared up at him. "Isn't it obvious?"

"I gotta go with Sky on this one," Josie whispered. "It's pretty hard to miss."

"I think Captain Jack was going for rhetorical," I whispered back.

"Oh."

"Where did you get the spear gun?" Captain Jack said, his eyes flaring.

"Uh, I found it on the boat," Sky said. "It was sitting near the snorkeling equipment. And you said we should help ourselves."

"To the snorkeling gear, you idiot. You saw the speargun, and you just thought you'd take it?" Captain Jack said, his voice rising an octave. "Get him on the boat."

We gently worked Sky to the stern, then helped him out of the water. After he had stretched out, dripping blood all over the boat, the four of us climbed aboard and removed our diving gear. Captain Jack, too angry to speak, leaned over Sky to examine the damage, then stood up and shook his head.

"You are one lucky son of a gun," he said, rummaging through a toolbox.

"I beg to differ, Captain," Sky said, inspecting his wound.

Captain Jack returned with a pair of metal cutters and cut the spear in two as close to the shoulder as he could. He tossed the long piece of the spear aside, then he opened a first aid kit and removed a tube of antiseptic cream and some bandages.

"You're lucky because it only hit muscle. It doesn't look like there's any tendon damage, and it definitely didn't hit bone." Captain Jack nodded at Bill. "Hold this idiot still while I pull it out."

"You sure you want to do that, Captain?" Sky said, flinching when Bill gently wrapped an arm around his neck.

"Well, I used the spear gun all day yesterday and didn't get around to cleaning it. If you want to run the risk of fish guts and bacteria getting into your bloodstream, just let me know. I'll be happy to leave it in there."

"Is it going to hurt?" Sky said, staring up at Captain Jack like a scared little boy.

"Oh, you can count on it," Captain Jack said, leaning down.

Despite his anger, Captain Jack gently wiggled what was left of the spear back and forth, then grabbed the spear tip and pulled it forward. Moments later, he handed the object to Henry who tossed it into a trash bin. A stream of blood oozed from the wound, and Captain Jack packed it tight with bandages then wrapped tape around Sky's shoulder. Then he stood and examined his work. Sky sat up, seemed to be waiting for it to hurt a lot more than it did, then nodded.

"That's not so bad," Sky said. "Thanks."

"Don't mention it," Captain Jack said, his anger again bubbling up. "Why did you think it was okay to take the spear gun without asking?"

"Because he was afraid he'd say no," Josie whispered to me.

"I was afraid you'd say no," Sky said.

"Told you," Josie said.

I punched her on the arm, and she glared at me and rubbed the spot.

"Of course, I would have said no," Captain Jack said. "And do you know why?"

"Because you were afraid somebody might do something stupid?" Sky said.

"Taking it was something stupid. I would have said no because somebody could have been killed."

"I'm sorry. You're right. It was a stupid thing to do. I just wanted to try it out and see what it's like."

"Now, you know," Captain Jack said. "Mission accomplished."

"Yeah, I guess. But it would probably be a lot more fun spearing a fish."

Captain Jack stared down at Sky, then shook his head and softened his tone a bit.

"How the heck did you end up shooting yourself in the shoulder?"

"I didn't," Sky said. "I dropped the spear gun, and then about a minute later, I got shot."

That bit of news gave all of us pause, and I let it roll around in my head. Nothing that made any sense returned, so I stayed quiet.

"It was weird," Sky said. "I figured it was long gone, and I was already trying to figure out a way to tell you I'd lost your spear gun when I felt a sharp pain in my shoulder."

"That's odd," Captain Jack said, frowning. "I guess it must have dropped onto the reef and hit something that caused it to discharge."

I glanced at Josie to see if she was buying the explanation. She looked back at me and shrugged. That pretty much summed up my reaction as well. Definitely weird, but probably accidental.

"Well, I'm so glad you're okay," Sally said. "But how about you stay away from spear guns in the future?"

"Yeah, I think I'll stick to painting."

"What were you doing when you got shot?" I said.

"What do you think we were doing?" Sky said, confused. "We were snorkeling."

"I meant at the exact time you got shot," I said. "Were you actually snorkeling at the time, or were you treading water?"

"What difference does that make?" Bill said, frowning.

"Probably none," I said, shrugging.

"We were definitely snorkeling at the time," Sally said.

"Yeah, no doubt about it," Sky said, nodding.

"I hate to do this, folks," Captain Jack said. "But we're going to need to get this guy to the emergency room."

"Of course," my mother said.

"But after we drop him off, we can head right back out if you like."

"I don't know," my mother said, glancing around at us. "What do you think, darling?"

"Gee, Mom. There's an awful lot of blood in the water," I said, then turned to Captain Jack. "How long does blood in the water hang around?"

"Well, it's hard to say," Captain Jack said, shrugging. "Probably for a while."

"Let me ask it this way. Would *you* go back in the water after something like that happened?"

"Absolutely not," Captain Jack blurted, then caught himself. "But that's just me."

"I'm seeing a day lounging around the pool in our future," I said, glancing around.

"Works for me," Josie said.

Everyone else nodded, and Captain Jack returned to the captain's chair and headed for shore. A few minutes later, we docked, and Sally helped Sky down the dock and into her car. We waved goodbye, then watched Bill and Captain Jack lift the ice chest onto the dock. Josie looked down at the chest, then over at me.

"I suppose you'd like a hand with that?" I deadpanned.

"Sure, now you're hungry and more than happy to help," Josie said as she grabbed one of the handles.

"Are you going to whine, or do you want to get out of here and have some lunch?"

"I could eat."

Chapter 23

When my mother had casually mentioned the memorial service for Jerome Crenshaw, I don't think she ever expected us to agree to go with her. And thinking back on it, I'm not even sure she actually invited us to go along in the first place. But when I eagerly took her up on her offer, she was a bit confused at first, then put it together and gave me a knowing smile.

"Okay, I get it, Snoopmeister. Just promise me you'll try to be on your best behavior."

"Of course, Mom. I'm just going to pay my respects. That's all," I said, hoping to slip the little white lie past her.

"Okay," she said. "But sit in the back and try to stay quiet."

Josie entered the living room wearing a cotton floral dress she'd bought yesterday when we'd gone shopping for funeral clothes. It stopped just above her knees, and she twirled back and forth looking down at it.

"I still don't know about this dress," she said. "Are you sure it's okay? I feel like I should be heading to brunch instead of a memorial service."

"Relax, dear," my mother said. "You're in the Caymans. And it's simply too hot for black."

"If you say so," Josie said, sitting down next to Chef Claire who was similarly attired.

After another short round of instructions from my mother about all of us behaving ourselves, we headed outside and found Henry already waiting for us. My mother had decided that showing up in a jeep wasn't appropriate, so we all piled into her Cadillac for the short drive to the church.

"Have you spoken with Gerald lately, Mom?"

"I talk to Gerald all the time, darling. Spoken to him about what?"

"About who might have killed Crenshaw. And Wily, too, now that I'm thinking about it."

"I'm afraid Gerald has bigger problems to worry about at the moment," she said, glancing over her shoulder at me.

"Like what?"

"Like keeping his job," she said, glancing over at Henry who was driving.

"What? Why on earth would he lose his job?" I said, feeling a rush of adrenaline. "This place is rolling in cash, right?"

"Let's just say that Crenshaw's death has created a few problems and leave it at that."

"You know I can't do that, Mom."

Josie and Chef Claire snorted. I grinned as I glanced back and forth at them.

"C'mon, Mom. Spill it."

"Jerome Crenshaw was a central player in many projects down here," my mother said.

"Yeah, I kinda figured that out. I saw the house, remember?"

"And since he was such a major player, his death has created a bit of a void."

"Why on earth would that cause a problem for Gerald?" I said, nodding to myself for asking what seemed to be a very logical question.

"Because it happened on his watch," my mother said, again glancing over her shoulder.

"He's the Finance Minister," I said. "If anybody was going to be blamed for it happening on their watch, wouldn't it be the police?"

My mother and Henry chuckled and grinned at each other.

"The police? Darling, you've been here a few days now. You must have figured out a few things about how this place works by now."

"If I'd been paying the least bit of attention to it, maybe," I said, not liking her patronizing tone. "I'm on vacation, Mom."

"Yes, we are," Josie deadpanned. "And it's going swimmingly well, wouldn't you say?"

"I know I'll never forget it," Chef Claire said.

"Shut it," I said. "Why would Gerald be held responsible for Crenshaw's murder?"

"Not his murder, darling. His death."

"Tomato, tomahto."

"Not in this case, darling. I'm afraid there's a huge difference."

"You lost me, Mom," I said, leaning forward.

"It's very complicated."

"Well, I would love to hear the story."

"Yes, darling. I'm sure you would."

Henry parked near the church, and he and my mother waved to several people as we made our way inside. I stopped near the entrance and looked up at the structure.

"Catholic, right?" I said to Josie.

"Yeah. You remember all the rules?"

"I think so," I said, following my mother toward the entrance. "I just hope they go nice and slow during the sit, stand, kneel part."

"Just follow my lead," Josie said, laughing.

"Lord, give me strength," my mother said, glancing skyward.

As instructed, we sat in a pew near the back, and my mother settled in then turned to look at us.

"Now, behave yourself."

"Geez, Mom. Give it a rest. Do you think I'm twelve?"

"Maybe on a good day," she said. "And no shenanigans like the last funeral we were at."

"When was that?" Josie whispered.

"Calducci's funeral," I said.

"Oh, yeah," Josie said. "That's when Fatal Franny threatened to track down and kill his murderer during her eulogy. That was a hoot."

"Yeah, she was on fire that day," I said.

Then I noticed Henry giving us a very strange look.

"What's on your mind, Henry?"

"You must lead very interesting lives," he said.

"It has its moments," I said, nodding.

"Well, let's hope this isn't one of them," my mother said.

I sat back and studied the large group. The church was overflowing, and a soft murmur echoed. Then I noticed Gerald escorting the widow Gloria to her seat in the front row. He had one hand on her back, the other on her elbow, and I wasn't sure if he was holding her up because of her grief, or if she had spent the morning drinking heavily. I nudged Josie and nodded at them as they continued walking down the aisle.

"What do you think?" I whispered.

"You mean, is she grief-stricken or just hammered?" she whispered back.

"Yeah."

"I gotta go with both."

"Yeah, me too. She's got that walleyed look that's usually associated with copious amounts of alcohol."

"Copious? Well, look at who's been brushing up on her vocabulary."

"Will you two please knock it off?" my mother whispered through tight lips.

I sat back and folded my hands in my lap. We watched Gerald help Gloria into her seat, then he sat down next to her.

"Are the two of them close?" I said to my mother.

"No, they hate each other," she whispered.

"Interesting. So, he's just being attentive as part of his official duties?"

"Yes. Now please be quiet."

"Promise me you'll tell me the whole story later, and you won't hear another word out of me."

"Oh, well played," Josie whispered.

"Thanks."

"All right, darling. I'll tell you the story. Anything to shut you up."

"Promise?"

My mother grabbed my forearm and pinched it hard.

"Ow. That wasn't necessary. Geez, lighten up, Mom."

"Young lady, I swear I'm about to drag you outside by your hair."

I rubbed my arm in silence and stayed relatively quiet for the rest of the service. I'd gotten a *young lady* out of her, and that was always dangerous ground to tread. And if I wanted to hear the rest of the story, I didn't want to press my luck. So, I sat back and listened to several eulogies, including a short, slurred one from the widow, that extolled the virtues of one Jerome Crenshaw. An hour later, after hearing about what a wonderful, generous, smart, funny, and charming fellow he was, my stomach was grumbling, and I was longing for a sandwich and a stroll on the beach.

And if several of the eulogies hadn't been received with suppressed snorts and giggles along with dozens of heads bowed to hide the smiles, my reaction might have been different.

But I did notice tears in Gerald's eyes during his short address to the mourners.

And I couldn't help wondering if the tears were for Crenshaw or for himself.

Chapter 24

On my way back from the garage where I'd spent an hour playing with the dogs, I saw Gerald and my mom sitting in the kitchen drinking coffee. They were in the middle of an intense conversation and didn't even look up, so I headed for my bedroom to change into my swimsuit. I tested myself for sunburn and was pleased to discover that I was now starting to develop a healthy-looking tan. I knew it didn't compare to my mom's, but my color was a whole lot better than the lily-white complexion I'd arrived with. But I knew that another sunburn was only one unprotected hour away, so I slathered myself with a sunscreen that had an SPF high enough to protect me from a nuclear meltdown. I tied my hair back, grabbed my hat and sunglasses, then headed for the pool to join Josie and Chef Claire. I walked back into the kitchen and stopped when I saw Gerald sitting by himself. He was staring off into space but smiled when he saw me.

"Going for a swim?"

"Nothing gets past you," I said, laughing.

"That's what I used to think," he said, shaking his head. "Your mother is on the phone. Oh, I've got an update on the dogs. As long as they get checked out by a local veterinarian before you go, nobody is going to give you a problem on your flight out. But they'll need all their shots, and…look who I'm talking to. I'm sure you know the drill."

"Yeah, we can figure all that out," I said, sitting down across from him. "We were just worried we might have a problem with immigration."

"No, you'll be fine," he said. "But if anybody does start asking a bunch of questions or giving you a hard time, feel free to drop my name. Or just call me."

"Thanks, Gerald. It must nice to have that much clout."

"Yeah," he whispered. "It must be nice."

"What's going on, Gerald?"

I made eye contact and held it.

"Wow. Right to the point, huh? Just like your mother."

"Yeah, probably. I really gotta work on that," I deadpanned.

He laughed and got up to refill his coffee. He extended the pot toward me, and I shook my head no. He sat back down and returned my stare.

"Questions?"

"Geez, where do I start?"

"Your call," he said, taking a sip of coffee.

"Okay, let's start with the one about why you're in danger of losing your job."

"You sure you don't want to start with something easy? Like the weather. Go ahead, ask me if I think it's going to rain."

It was my turn to laugh, and I got up and grabbed a bottle of water from the fridge.

"So, what's the deal with your job?"

"I could lose my job because of what might happen to Majestic Vista," he said.

"Catchy name. What is it?"

"It's the biggest high-end real estate development project that's ever been undertaken on the island."

"I see. And I assume we're talking about houses like the Crenshaw's?"

"Nothing quite that majestic," he said, chuckling. "But you get the idea."

"And now that Crenshaw is dead, the project's in jeopardy?"

"It is."

"Because the widow is threatening to pull out, right?"

"How on earth did you know that?" he said, his eyes narrowing. "Did your mother say something?"

"No, she didn't say a word," I said, taking a sip of water.

"Then how did you know?"

"I got the idea when we were at the memorial service. I saw you helping Gloria down the aisle to her seat and asked my mother if the two of you were close. She said you hated each other."

"We do," he said, nodding. "She's an unstable, chronic alcoholic who was given everything in life."

"So, I take it you and Gloria never made any memories?"

"Oh, we share lots of memories. And all of them bad. But to address your rather intrusive observation, no, Gloria and I never made any of those memories. I don't go to those parties."

"But you were at the one the other night," I said, raising an eyebrow.

"Yes, I went with your mother. We were planning on having a conversation with Gloria, but that obviously didn't happen."

"My mother is involved in Majestic Vista?"

"Of course," he said, nodding. "You seem surprised to hear that."

"Maybe a little. She never mentioned it."

"Your mother can be very secretive when it comes to her financial affairs," Gerald said. "I think it's because she doesn't want anyone to know how much money she actually has."

"You could have fooled me. She certainly likes to spend it," I said.

Gerald found my comment very funny, and he laughed hard.

"She couldn't come close to spending it all if she tried," he said. "You do know how much she's worth, don't you?"

"Yeah, I've seen the numbers," I said, frowning. "I'm not comfortable talking about it."

"Just like your mother."

"Will you please stop saying that?"

"You should be honored to be compared to her," he said, giving me a fatherly look.

"Yeah, I am," I said, nodding, then I patted his hand. "Just don't tell her that, okay?"

"Your secret's safe with me."

I sat quietly for a long time and waited for the lightbulb to come on. Eventually, it flickered.

"Crenshaw was the biggest investor in the project, wasn't he?"

"Yes, he was. By far."

Gerald headed to the fridge for a bottle of water. He also grabbed a container of fresh fruit and set it down between us. I munched on a chunk of pineapple as I formulated my next question. The lightbulb flickered again, then held.

"He invested in Majestic Vista without his wife's knowledge, didn't he?"

"Well done. Your reputation is well deserved," he said.

"Thanks. I have my moments. I imagine that Gloria didn't appreciate her husband spending that much of her money without asking. And when she found out, she went ballistic."

"To say the least, yes," Gerald said, scanning the container of fruit before selecting a slice of mango.

"And now she plans to pull out and kill the deal?"

"Even worse," he said. "She's threatening to challenge the legality of the contract."

"She wants to tie the project up in court?"

"Yeah."

"Geez, that's diabolical," I said, grabbing another piece of pineapple. "This is delicious."

"That's Gloria."

"And if her lawyer is any good, which I assume is a given, the right kind of injunction would freeze the deal as it is and nobody will be able to get their money out until it's settled. My guess is that Gloria will try to string it out for years if she can."

"You're incredible," he said, giving me a look of admiration. "How would you like to come down here and work for me?"

"Would there be dogs involved?"

"No," he said, laughing.

"Then I'll pass," I said, smiling at him. Then I had a thought that worried me. "My mother isn't in over her head on this thing, is she?"

"No, your mother is way too smart to do something stupid like that. And she'll either eventually get all her money back, or make a bunch more if the project does get built."

"I guess she didn't make all that money by doing stupid stuff."

"Unfortunately, some of our other investors aren't as smart as your mother."

"And they invested everything they had in the project?"

"Yes. And a few of them even borrowed more from the banks just so they could get a bigger share of the profits."

"Ouch."

"Indeed."

"And now Gloria has everyone right where she wants them," I said.

"Yes. Our male investors are calling it the death grip. I'm sure you get the image."

"Yeah, I got it," I said, nodding. "It's brilliant on her part. Absolutely vindictive, but brilliant."

"I'm sorry, but I don't share that opinion," he said, shaking his head. "But I will concede the vindictive part. She's a dreadful human being."

"I'll take your word for it," I said, reaching for a slice of mango. "But she didn't kill her husband."

"Why do you say that?"

"Because if she is that spiteful, there is no way she would have killed him. That would take away a lot of her fun. If he was around while the project was tied up in court, Jerome would have been a pariah around here. And she'd be able to use it against him every single day. You know, keep the wound nice and fresh."

"Exactly. And now you understand the nature of my problem," he said, drumming his fingers on the marble.

"You're not one of the investors, are you?"

"No, as a government official, the *Finance Minister*, there is no way I could be an investor in the project. At least, directly," he said, raising an eyebrow.

"Got it," I said, nodding. "But your *indirect* involvement is substantial, isn't it?"

"Yes. I'm the one who pretty much put the investment group together. My fingerprints are all over the deal. I personally supervised all the contracts and associated paperwork, and…how do you say it?"

"Greased the skids?"

"Yes."

"And they're pretty greasy, right?"

"Well, they certainly were," he said, managing a small laugh. "But if the project does get tied up in the courts, it's going to be a major embarrassment for the government. Not to mention the fact that they'll be a whole lot of important people walking around very unhappy. Someone is going to have to pay for creating the problem. And that someone is going to be me."

"No good deed goes unpunished, right?"

"Your mother said the exact same thing."

"She stole it from me," I said, grinning. "Was there any opposition to the project? You know, someone who could have killed Crenshaw to stop it from being built?"

"Well, we always have some people complaining about the ongoing commercial development of the islands," he said, shrugging.

"From what I've seen of the place, it's a little late to start worrying about that now, isn't it?"

"Yes, that's what we all thought," he said.

"Would the project cause a lot of displacement for folks who live here?"

"Not really," he said. "The land is pretty much vacant."

"I guess it's possible that one or more of your investors wanted to stop the deal in its current form and see if they could get a bigger slice of the pie," I said, thinking out loud.

"That's my working theory at the moment. And your mother agrees with me."

"No, that's not it," I said, immediately discarding my suggestion. "If the investors are that worried about their cash flow, they wouldn't do something like that."

"Maybe they just didn't think through all the possible ramifications," Gerald said.

"No, at least one of them would have seen this coming," I said. "It's not that hard to see. I figured it out in about a minute and a half, and my financial skills wouldn't fill this fruit bowl."

"Maybe you're right."

"But I suppose it could have been one rogue investor who doesn't care what happens to anybody else," I said. "Was Wily one of the investors?"

"He was."

"How about the boring guy at dinner?"

"Timothy?"

"Yeah."

"No, he did some work for us, but he wasn't one of the investors."

"Did he want to be?"

"I'm sure he did," Gerald said. "Anyone who got a look at the numbers would definitely want in."

"Interesting."

"Timothy? A killer? No way. He's afraid of his own shadow."

"How about Bill and Jerry?"

"No, they weren't involved in the project. We actually offered it to them, but they said it was a bit too rich for their blood. They thought about it, then decided to pass."

"How about other major investors on the island? Are there any of them walking around grumpy because they weren't included?"

"I don't think so," he said, shaking his head. "If there were, I would have heard about it."

"Because you're the Finance Minister, right?"

"For now."

My mother entered the kitchen and grabbed a piece of pineapple.

"What are we talking about?" she said, glancing back and forth at us.

"Majestic Vista," I said.

"I would have thought you'd be talking about who killed Wily and Crenshaw," she said, grabbing a second piece.

"We were," I said, glancing at Gerald. "Indirectly."

Chapter 25

I propped myself up on my elbows on the towel and watched Chef Claire and the dogs. They were at the edge of the water, and the puppies were doing their best to figure out why the water kept going back and forth under their paws. The bloodhound was playing fetch with Chef Claire while the basset kept a watchful eye on her brood.

"How many do you think will get adopted?" Josie said, rummaging through the cooler between us for a beer.

"I'm not sure. But it doesn't really matter, does it?" I said, glancing over at her.

"No," she said, laughing as she handed me one of the ice-cold cans. "And I want to keep the bloodhound. I've gotten attached to him."

"Nice. Just what we need around the house. Another big dog," I said, shaking my head.

"He'll fit right in."

"Yes, he certainly will."

"Did you call the Inn this morning?" Josie said.

"Right after I got up. Everything's fine. Sammy said that Captain and Chloe are missing us."

"Well, they better be. You didn't mention that they'll be responsible for running the place during the winter, did you?"

"No, I thought we'd surprise them with the news when we got back," I said, taking a sip of beer.

"You sure you want to do this?"

"I think so. Don't you?"

"I can think of worse ways to spend the winter," Josie said. "I am a bit worried about Captain spending all that time in this heat."

"Between the pool and the air conditioning, I'm sure he'll be fine."

"He and Chloe are going to love the ocean," she said. "You do know that your mom might want us to live with her."

"I'm way ahead of you," I said, laughing. "And that's where Captain comes in."

"All that sand," she said, grinning.

"Yeah, it would take her about a week before she'd *gently suggest* that we find our own place."

"You're diabolical," Josie said.

"There seems to be a lot of that going around. But we won't be living with her," I said, draining the rest of my beer. "Wow, that didn't take long."

"It's really hot, and the beer's really cold," she said, shrugging. "And you're on vacation."

"Excellent points. I'll have another."

"Do you think we'll be able to find someplace to rent down here?" she said, handing me a fresh beer.

"Since we're going to be spending at least three months a year down here, I was talking with my mom, and she thought we should probably buy a place."

"Have you seen the prices of real estate on this island?"

"I have," I said, staring out at the ocean. "But we'd never lose money on it. I'm trying to think of it as an investment."

"Do you have several million laying around I don't know about?" she said, tossing her empty can into the cooler.

"No, but my mother does," I whispered.

"Wow. Listen to you."

"What?"

"You're actually going to let your mother help you without putting up a fight. Good for you."

"I was thinking about it all last night," I said.

"I knew I smelled something burning down the hall."

"Shut it. Something Gerald said yesterday got me thinking."

"I'm sure he said a lot of things that got you thinking."

"Yeah, he did. But he said that my mother couldn't spend everything she has even if she tried."

"And that was news to you?" Josie said, cracking the top on a fresh beer.

"No, it was more of a reminder. And when I put that together with the fact that she's one of the investors in that project, I decided why not? She's constantly dabbling in real estate and always on the lookout for a way to make more money. And she's dying to get us down here. So, if she's willing to buy a house for us to live in, and keep it in her own name, we could rent it back from her."

"It would be a whole lot simpler if you'd just take the money," Josie said, shaking her head.

"Yeah, I know. But I'm not there yet," I said.

"Well, this is certainly a big step in the right direction."

I got up off the towel and brushed myself off. Then I slipped into my shorts.

"Are you going somewhere?" Josie said, squinting up at me.

"I thought we'd go take a look at that vacant house up the beach."

"The one where we first spotted Bailey?"

"Yup, that's the one. My mother told me this morning that it's for sale," I said, rocking back and forth on my heels as I jingled a set of keys.

"You're kidding, right?"

"Nope."

"Geez, she's good. She set the whole thing up."

"Yeah, I'm sure she did," I said. "We should have seen it coming. Her plan was to get us down here, and it had to include a place for us to live."

"So, she doesn't want us living with her?"

"I think she thinks she does," I said. "But she said she's going to buy the place regardless. She said it's a steal."

"And here I thought we might buy one of the houses at Majestic Vista," Josie deadpanned.

"If we did, you'd be living there by yourself. C'mon. Let's grab Chef Claire and get the dogs settled in. Then we'll go take a look at the place."

"Unbelievable," she said. "And to think, I was more than happy just sitting on the beach having a couple of beers."

"Yeah, well, my mother would never be happy just doing that."

"That's probably why she's got all that money."

Chapter 26

For three people who were supposed to be on vacation, we sure were busy. Given that we only had a few days left, our to-do list was long and growing, and it was either take care of a few big items or immediately start making plans for a return trip. And to combat the stress that was starting to work its way into our systems, we decided to divide up the task list between us.

At the top of the list was the well-being of the dogs, and Josie volunteered to make sure the dogs had all their shots and paperwork in order. She located a local vet, enlisted Henry's assistance, and they headed for her office with all the dogs in tow. Chef Claire was responsible for scouting possible locations for the restaurant. Since she was the only one with a clue about what was required to run a restaurant, it was an easy decision to assign that one to her. She contacted a few commercial real estate agents, did some online research of her own, then headed off to meet with one of the agents and take a look at a couple of properties she thought might work.

Since I was now officially, as Josie called it, obsessed with the murders, both she and Chef Claire knew that I'd be pretty much useless dealing with anything else. And I must admit I was a bit hurt when they both enthusiastically agreed to divvy up the tasks when I first suggested it. The prospect of getting away for a while from my increasingly annoying what-if questions, apparently, had been too enticing to pass up. And my hurt feelings shifted into annoyance when they both drove a little too fast down the driveway earlier with wide grins.

Fortunately, I was assigned an easy task. Easy in that it was pointless to worry about doing a good job since it fell into the uncontrollable category. I was assigned to my mother and the new house. Ever since I had told her that we were interested in her idea, she'd developed a level of excitement and focus that, to be kind, was completely over the top. Other possible descriptors include unbearable, insufferable, and smothering, but, since this is my mother we're talking about, I'm cutting her a break. At first, I'd tried to hold my own with her, and we'd gone back and forth for an hour arguing about her initial plans with the house. When Josie laughingly mentioned that my mother's behavior was starting to remind her of someone else she knew, my feelings again were hurt initially, and I fell silent and pouted. But then I realized what a break I'd caught.

Right after breakfast, my mother grabbed the keys to the vacant property and a tape measure, then strolled down the beach to measure the windows for curtains. Given that the house had more windows that we had dogs, I figured I had at least a couple of hours to work on the murders, so I begged off and headed out to the pool for a morning swim.

People were always trying to convince me that vigorous exercise was a great way to stay sharp mentally, so I decided to give it a shot. As I did laps, I forced my mind to go blank and was determined to keep swimming until my thoughts coalesced around something useful. But after six laps, I was breathing heavily, and I convinced myself that I always did my best thinking when relaxed. I climbed out of the pool, toweled off, then stretched out on a lounge chair and promptly fell asleep.

I woke up a few minutes later with an idea bouncing around in my head. It definitely wasn't the best idea I ever had, but it was a start. And it sure beat swimming laps. I grabbed my phone, called Gerald at his office, and asked him for the number. Once he got past his initial surprise and several questions, he gave me the number. I made the call, again got past the initial surprise and some more questions, then headed inside to shower and change.

A half-hour later, I pulled into the massive circular driveway in front of the Crenshaw's house and headed up the front steps. I looked around, dwarfed by the massive entrance, then rang the bell. I'd expected a servant to answer the door but was surprised to see Gloria Crenshaw standing in front of me when it opened.

"Ms. Chandler, right?"

"Suzy. It's nice to see you again, Mrs. Crenshaw."

"We've met before?" she said, frowning.

"Yes. At the barbecue the night your husband was…well, you know."

She searched her memory bank, but came up empty and shook her head.

"I'm sorry, I don't remember. But I was pretty hammered. Come in."

She escorted me down a very long hallway, and I half-expected to see a registration area bustling with staff and guests checking in. She stopped in a large sunroom off the industrial-sized kitchen and gestured at an overstuffed chair that greeted me affectionately when I sat down.

"This is really comfortable," I said, wiggling back and forth.

"I'm glad you like it," she said, sitting down across from me and lighting a cigarette. "You said something about figuring out who killed my husband?"

"At the moment, it's more of a notion, I think," I said, glancing around. "Your house is amazing. Would you mind if I take a few photos before I go? The folks back home will never believe this place."

"There's no need for that," she said, reaching down for a magazine sitting on the coffee table between us and handing it to me. "That's an extra copy. Keep it."

I stared at the cover photo, a panoramic overhead shot of the house that must have been taken from a helicopter. Then I flipped through several pages of interior shots that included the sunroom I was sitting in.

"I didn't want to agree to the photo shoot," Gloria said. "But Jerome talked me into it."

"This is a very famous magazine," I said. "I'm impressed. Thanks for the copy."

"Don't mention it," she said, already bored with the conversation. Then she glanced up and smiled. "Oh, there you are. Right on time. Thanks, Maggie."

"Here you go, Mrs. Crenshaw," the woman said. "A Bloody Mary just the way you like it. I also brought one for your friend." She set the drink down in front of me and smiled. "I hope you can force one of these down."

"Don't worry," Gloria said, taking a big gulp of hers. "If she doesn't want it, it won't go to waste."

"Of course," Maggie said, then performed what looked like a half-bow, half-curtsy and headed off.

"I have to get her to stop doing that," Gloria said. "Jerome thought the staff needed to be a bit more...oh, what's the word I'm looking for?"

"Colonial?"

She laughed then drained half of her drink.

"I was thinking along the lines of subservient, but that'll do. Colonial. I must remember that."

I sipped my Bloody and flinched. Whoever the morning bartender was had used a heavy hand with the vodka. Before I could speak, Maggie strolled back into the room and set two more drinks down on the table in front of us.

"There you go, Mrs. Crenshaw. Will there be anything else at the moment?"

"No, we're good, Maggie. Thanks."

Gloria drained what was left of her first drink. She rattled the ice, tipped the glass and her head back to get any last drops, then placed the empty glass on the silver tray Maggie was holding. She left the sunroom, and Gloria sighed as the vodka began working its magic. She took a sip from the fresh Bloody, then sat back and draped one leg over the other.

"So, you're here to talk about my husband's murder?"

"Yes."

"But you aren't with the police? On the phone, you mentioned something about running a hotel for dogs."

"Well, the hotel is only one part of the business," I said. "But, yes, that's what I do for a living."

"Would you mind explaining how that qualifies you to work on a murder case?"

"It's kind of a hobby," I said, shrugging.

"I see. And you thought you'd just pop in to see if you could figure out if I killed my husband?"

"No," I said, shaking my head. "I know you didn't kill your husband."

"Really? Then you're the first person I've talked to since he died who doesn't," she said, studying me closely. "Why don't you think I killed that worthless waste of oxygen?"

"Well, I have a theory," I said, frowning. "But I don't know if I should mention it."

"No, please. I'd love to hear it."

"Okay, and I'm going to apologize right up front for possibly offending you. I don't think you killed him because you thought that would be going too easy on him."

"Interesting," she said, nodding. "Please, continue."

"After you learned about Majestic Vista, I'm sure you were very upset with him."

"Funny," she said, smiling. "You don't seem to be the type of person prone to understatement."

"Yeah, well, I'm trying to be gentle," I said, smiling back. "When you heard about the project, I imagine you probably were mad enough to kill him."

"In all honesty, the thought did cross my mind."

"But if you did, then you wouldn't be able to use it against him in the future. Doing what he did without his wife's permission was beyond the pale. At least, in my opinion, it was. You would have been able to remind him about it for a very long time. That would have given you some serious leverage in your marriage. If you're into that sort of thing."

"Well, what would you have done if you found out your husband had invested a hundred million of your money without your knowledge?"

"I probably would have killed him," I said, glancing at her over the top of my glass. "But that's just me."

Gloria roared with laughter and choked on a piece of ice. She coughed several times, then wiped her mouth with a napkin.

"You're good," she said. "Insightful and funny."

"I have my moments."

"Okay, if I didn't kill my husband, what's your theory on who did?"

"I'm sure it was someone who was at my mother's house the night Wily was killed."

"Ah, yes. Wily."

"How well did you know him?"

"Wily? Well enough to know to stay away from him. He was a regular at those ridiculous parties my husband organized. Wily and my husband liked to hang out and compare notes."

"Notes on all the women they'd been with?"

"Of course."

"And did you and Wily ever…you know…make a memory?"

"Of course not. He was a disgusting human being. And for the record, I hated those parties. And whenever we had one, I'd start drinking early in the day so I could be passed out by the time the party got rolling."

"If you hated the parties so much, why on earth did you tolerate them?"

"My husband was convinced it was the best way to get the information he needed for his business."

"Real estate development, right?"

"Yes. Among other things. Look, you need to understand something. My husband was never comfortable with the fact that all of our money was mine. At least it was early on when we first got married. He felt emasculated by my money and was determined to make enough of his own to justify this lifestyle. Apart from his considerable flaws and shortcomings, he was blessed with a very strong work ethic."

"I see. That makes sense," I said, nodding. "You said the police think you killed him."

"Yes, but they don't seem to be working too hard to confirm it. But if that's what they want to believe, so be it. I was passed out in bed when it happened."

"Did the police discuss the murder weapon with you?"

"Oh, the infamous *skewer*," she said, laughing. "Of course. When I reminded them that Wily had been killed the same way, they said that I could have used it as a way of deflecting attention away from me. I didn't even know how Wily had been killed until I heard some people discussing it at the party."

"The skewer does set up an interesting twist," I said.

"Twist? Don't you think the same person committed both murders?" she said, then glanced down at my untouched Bloody Mary. "Are you going to drink that?"

"No, it's all yours," I said. "Maybe twist isn't the right word. Coincidence? No, that's not it. Parallel? No. I'm not doing a very good job with this, am I?"

"Well, you are on vacation," she said, gesturing for me to get on with it.

"Sure, sure. At first, I didn't think it was the same person. But I do now. The same person but for different reasons."

She took a sip and thought about my comment. Then she shrugged it off.

"I'm not sure it really matters. So, how can I help you?"

"I'd like to invite you to dinner at my mom's house tomorrow night."

"What?"

"It's sort of a going away dinner for us. We're heading home, and I thought it would be good to get everyone back together who was there the night Wily got killed."

"Why would I do that? I detest all of those people. Apart from your mother. She's the only one I actually enjoy being around."

"Yeah, I get that," I said. "Some of them aren't my favorite people either. But I think it will help confirm who killed your husband."

"Confirm? You think you know who did it?"

"I'm pretty sure. But I'm going to need some proof."

"And you need me there?"

"Yes, I do."

"To do what?"

"To announce that you're going to drop your case against Majestic Vista."

"What? Those people were trying to get their hooks into a hundred million of my money."

"Yes, I know. Just tell them the deal is off, and if you get all your money back, you'll call off your attack dogs."

"And that, by itself, is going to confirm who killed Jerome and Wily?"

"Well, that's my working theory at the moment. I'm going to need to grease the skids a bit more, but I think it'll work."

"I don't know," she said through a crocodile smile that made me nervous. "I was really looking forward to screwing with those snakes. I could make their lives miserable for a very long time."

"Without a doubt," I said. "But I'm sure you have better ways to spend your time."

"Actually, I don't," she said, frowning. "But I would like to know who killed my husband. Okay, I'll play. But if the killer isn't revealed, I'm going ahead as planned."

"Fair enough," I said, getting up from my chair. "Seven o'clock tomorrow night. Does that work for you?"

"I'll be there. Should I bring anything?"

"Just a high tolerance for the mundane."

"And my sense of humor?"

"Why not? It couldn't hurt."

Chapter 27

We'd been debating how to spend our last day in the sun when my mother suggested that we call Bill and Jerry. As two locals who knew their way around better than most, she thought they'd have some good suggestions. And since I was looking for any opportunity to talk with people who'd been at my mother's house the night Wily was murdered, I readily agreed to make the call. When Bill and Jerry suggested another boat trip, we thought a nice relaxing day on the water with food and drink sounded good. And since all three of us enjoyed their company, we decided to invite them along.

But now I was having my doubts when I saw Captain Jack slowly maneuver his boat into a shallow area dominated by sandbars and cut the engine. I glanced around at a large number of other watercraft and what appeared to be at least a couple hundred tourists wading in shallow water. I noticed dark shadows in the water I assumed were being caused by clouds partially blocking the sun and glanced up at a perfect blue sky. Confused, I looked at Bill and Jerry who were staring out at the water with huge fixed smiles.

"It never gets old, does it?" Bill said to his wife. "Mother nature at her finest."

"No, it's incredible," she said, staring out over the water. "We should do this more often."

"I agree," he said. "It really helps you develop an appreciation for how special this place is."

"But it's always so crowded out here," Jerry said.

"What are you gonna do, huh?" Bill said, shrugging.

"What are those dark shadows in the water?" I said.

"They're stingrays," Bill said, baffled by my question. "What else would they be?"

"I don't know. Maybe miniature stealth bombers?" I said, staring down into the water.

Bill and Jerry both laughed.

"Just like her mother," Jerry said.

"Yeah, I was just gonna say the same thing," he said.

I was too focused on the large objects lazily swimming around the tourists' legs to worry about, once again, being compared to my mother.

"How big do those things get?" I said.

Bill stretched his arms apart as far as they would go, and Jerry nodded.

"You're joking, right?" I said.

"Well, they're pretty well fed," Bill said, laughing.

"And people actually pay money to get in the water with them?" I said, frowning.

"Of course," Bill said.

"But they're wild creatures. How is this even possible?"

"It started decades ago when fisherman used to clean their daily catch in this area. They'd throw the fish guts and everything else they didn't want overboard into the shallow water around the sandbars. Eventually, the stingrays began congregating. They must have started associating the sound of a boat engine with food. Over time, people diving around here figured out that the stingrays could be fed by hand and then the inevitable happened."

"The whole area became a tourist attraction," I said.

"Yeah," Bill said, frowning. "It's what most people call progress. But what are you gonna do, right?"

"Take their money," I said.

"Exactly."

"What do they eat?"

"Chunks of squid," Jerry said, pointing at Captain Jack who was filling several small pails with what I assumed was the substance she was talking about.

"And you just wade around in the water and feed them?" I said.

"Yes. But don't worry, you won't have to walk very far. They'll find you and swim right up," Jerry said.

"I'm sorry, but that's exactly what I'm worried about. Couldn't I just feed them from the boat?"

"I guess you could," Bill said. "But what would be the point of that?"

"Self-preservation for a start. Those things can really hurt you, right?"

"Well, I already mentioned that you shouldn't try to pull on their tails," Bill said. "They have a barb on the end of it that will really get your attention if you touch it."

"Oh, don't worry. I haven't forgotten. But what about getting bit? They do have a mouth, don't they?"

Bill and Jerry again found my comment funny. They looked at each other, then Bill nodded for her to go ahead.

"Well, there is a fairly common *injury*, if you can call it that," she said, smiling.

"Oh, I'm pretty sure I'll be calling it an injury," I said, staring at her. "Spill it, Jerry."

"Some of the really tame stingrays, you know, ones that have lost all their fear of humans, will swim right up to you looking for a piece of squid. Once in a while, they miss the squid and make contact with the person trying to feed them."

"Okay," I said, frowning. "Now would probably be a good time for you to get to the injury part."

"Well, the stingrays suck the food into their mouth, and it's possible that you could end up with a…bit of a mark if they make contact with you."

"What?" I said, dumbfounded. "You're telling me one of those things might give me a *hickey*?"

"Unlikely," Jerry said, giving me a small smile. "But, yes, it's possible."

"You'll be fine," Bill said. "You've got a better chance of getting hit by lighting."

"Well, then just find me a thunderstorm, and I'll be more than happy to test your theory," I said, then glanced back at Josie and Chef Claire. "Are you getting all this?"

"Don't worry," Josie said. "Every word."

"I only have one question," Chef Claire said.

"What's that?"

"What on earth are we doing out here?"

"From the sound of it, Suzy's looking for a date," Josie deadpanned.

"Shut it." I turned to Bill and Jerry. "I can't believe you guys. You suggested a nice relaxing day out on a boat."

"We're on a boat," Bill said, giving me a blank stare.

"Yeah, I guess," I said, frowning. "If you want to get technical about it."

"And it's certainly a nice day," Jerry said. "And you are relaxed, right?"

"Well, I was."

"When you called and said you'd like to do something fun on your last day, we thought this would be perfect," Bill said.

"And you still had a half-day credit with Captain Jack because we had to cut our dive trip short the other day. When your mother suggested this, we thought it made perfect sense since it's one of our favorite things to do. And it's something everyone should experience."

"My mother, huh?"

"Yes. I thought she would have said something. But I guess she wanted to surprise you," Bill said.

"Mission accomplished," Josie said, climbing to her feet. "Okay, let's do this. Is there anything else we should know? You know, important safety tips, stuff like that?"

"Not really," Jerry said. "But you'll probably be surprised when you touch your first ray. Their skin sort of feels like sandpaper. Just try not to react too much."

"Yeah, just don't make any sudden moves and you'll be fine," Bill said.

"No worries about that," I said. "I usually don't move around much when I'm terrified."

Again, they both laughed. Apparently, I was at my funniest when humor was the last thing on my mind.

We stripped down to our swimsuits, then Captain Jack handed each of us a pail filled with chunks of squid. Josie glanced down at hers, then at Chef Claire.

"It looks different from the calamari we serve at the restaurant," she said.

"I'm sure the stingrays won't mind," Chef Claire said, glancing down at the slimy collection in her bucket. "Geez, that looks disgusting."

"You know," Captain Jack said, giving us a wicked grin that told us he was enjoying our discomfort way too much. "Instead of just wading through the water, you could go diving with them if you like. I've got all the gear."

"That's okay, Captain Jack," I said. "I'm going to have enough trouble breathing as it is."

"Okay, Cousteau," Josie said, gently shoving me toward the ladder. "Lead the way."

"Hey, don't push me," I said, glaring at her. "You sure you don't want to go first?"

"Yeah, right. Like that's going to happen."

"We'll go first," Bill said, grabbing the ladder. "Once you see how much fun we're having, I'm sure you'll want to jump right in."

"Sure, sure."

We watched them slide into the water and take a piece of squid from their buckets. They moved the chunks back and forth in the water, and a group of four stingrays began heading straight for them. We waited until they had both offered a half dozen pieces to the rays, checked to make sure they still had all their fingers, then slowly worked our way down the ladder.

I found solid footing on the sandy bottom and grimaced as I reached into my pail for a piece of the squid. I held it out in the water, noticed a stingray effortlessly gliding toward me, then panicked and dropped the squid. The chunk slowly drifted down then disappeared when the ray flashed by.

"Wow, they're fast when they want to be," I said to Josie who was standing a few feet away.

"Yeah," she said, keeping a close eye on two stingrays that were brushing up against her legs like they were old friends. "Hey, watch where you're going, buddy." She glanced over. "I guess this isn't so bad."

"Compared to what?" I said, still trying to prevent a full-on panic attack.

"Oh, there is one more thing I probably should have mentioned," Bill said as he casually fed a small group of rays that definitely liked what he was offering.

"Bill, I gotta say that you're not instilling a lot of confidence in me, I said, staring at him, wild-eyed. "What is it?"

"Try not to step on one of them," he said. "Sometimes they like to bury themselves in the sand, and they can be a little hard to see. So, just shuffle your feet when you walk, and you'll be fine."

"Don't you think that was something you should have mentioned before we got in the water?" I snapped.

"Hey, I'm sorry. I forgot. But just be careful, and you'll be fine."

I refocused on the stingrays that were slowly swimming around my legs. One of what Jerry had called the *tame* ones bumped into the side of my leg. And what ensued next seemed to last forever, although it couldn't have been more than a few seconds since it played out while I was underwater holding my breath.

I was surprised by the force of the impact and stumbled backward a couple of steps. I stepped on something, momentarily panicked, then realized as I began to fall, that I'd only stepped on a seashell. But before I could relax and find my balance, I fell backward and landed with a splash. I dropped my pail, and dozens of pieces of slimy squid surrounded me in the water. The stingrays must have thought that Christmas, or maybe Thanksgiving, had come early, and they began circling me and fighting for their fair share of the bounty. Frozen in fear, I sat down on the sandy bottom, closed my eyes, and tried to wait out the feeding frenzy.

Then I felt a weight on the top of my head. I snuck a quick peek and realized that one of the stingrays had decided to use my head as a place to sit while it snacked on the chunks floating near my face. Out of the corner of my eyes, I noticed the gentle flapping of gray, and it must have looked like I'd managed to grow elephant ears. Too terrified to reach up and push the stingray off my head, I shook my head vigorously, and the ray spooked and began to swim away.

I felt its tail bounce off my back, and, seconds later, I realized that the ray's barbed tail had sliced the string that held the top of my two-piece up. I opened my eyes and saw my top drifting toward the bottom. But any thought I had of trying to retrieve it disappeared when I saw a large stingray heading straight for a chunk of squid that was floating right in front of my face. My fear level rose off the chart, and I raised both hands above my head, then changed my mind when I decided that stingrays probably didn't understand the surrender signal, and covered my eyes with my hands. I tried to make myself as small as possible in the water, realized what a ridiculous idea that was, and then thought about trying to swat the stingray away. But I changed my mind again, raised my arms back over my head, then closed my eyes and held my breath.

Then I felt a short, intense tug on my right breast and I screamed at the top of my lungs and produced a long trail of air bubbles that drifted toward the surface. I flailed my arms in the water and scrambled to my feet. I popped up above the surface and saw the rest of the group staring at me like I'd lost my mind.

"What on earth is the matter?" Josie said.

"I'm injured," I said, examining my naked right breast.

All four stared at the deep red circular mark, then Bill, after taking a long admiring look, finally did the gentlemanly thing and looked away.

"Wow," Chef Claire said. "Bullseye."

"Yeah," Josie said, nodding. "Now, that's what I call a hickey."

"Geez, that hurts," I said, massaging my breast as I looked at Jerry. "Am I going to be okay?"

"You'll be fine," she said.

"Will you people please stop saying that?" I said, then glanced at Josie. "What do you think?"

"Well, I think you went a bit far for a first date, but what the heck, you are on vacation."

"You're really not funny."

"Disagree," Chef Claire said, laughing.

I waded back to the ladder, made my way up, and waited for Captain Jack to toss me my tee shirt before I climbed aboard.

"What happened?" Captain Jack said.

"I got bit," I snapped.

"It doesn't look like a bite."

"Actually, it was more of a suck."

"A stingray sucked your breast?"

"Yes. Can you believe that?"

"Well, maybe it was a young ray."

"What?"

"You know, one that was still nursing."

"Everybody's a comedian."

He looked away laughing at his own joke as I pulled my tee shirt over my head. Then I sat down and continued to massage my breast as I waited for the others to get back on the boat. Captain Jack started the boat, and we slowly made our way back to shore. He was still chuckling when he secured the lines and waved goodbye as the five of us made our way down the dock.

Then the three of us hopped into our jeep and headed for home trailed by Bill and Jerry in their car.

"Well, that was fun," Chef Claire said from the backseat.

"Oh, I can't wait to tell this story," Josie said, still laughing at the fresh memory.

"Sure, you can laugh. You're not the one who almost lost a nipple," I said, driving with one hand on the wheel. Then I took a deep breath and exhaled loudly. "Well, at least the day hasn't been a total disaster."

"Are you going to explain yourself, or do I have to wait?" Josie said.

"Are you going to make any more love bite jokes?"

"Oh, I'm sure of it."

"Then you're gonna have to wait."

Chapter 28

Freshly showered and with a generous dab of antiseptic cream rubbed into my wound, I stretched out on a lounge chair and watched Josie play tuggy with Bailey in the shallow end of the pool. She eventually gave up the battle and got out of the water. She headed for the house to shower and change followed closely by the bloodhound. Chef Claire and Henry were standing by the grill discussing, I assumed, cooking tips, while Bill and Jerry were sitting nearby sipping Mudslides and chatting quietly.

My mother appeared and strolled across the lawn toward us like she didn't have a care in the world. Which she probably didn't. As I often did, I watched her closely and wondered if I would be lucky enough to look as good as her when I got to that age. Then that got me thinking about mortality, and I immediately chased that subject away and went back to pouting about my injury. I subconsciously starting rubbing the tender spot on my breast and waved to my mother with my other hand. She stopped directly in front of my lounge chair and looked down at me.

"Hello, darling. I was going to stop by for a quick chat, but it looks like you'd rather be alone."

"Funny, Mom," I said, letting go of my breast.

"No bra tonight?" she said with a big grin. "Daring."

"No, chafing."

"I wish I could have been there," she said, laughing as she glanced off into the distance trying to picture the scene.

"Yeah, it was a real hoot. What's up?"

"I bought the house today," she said, sounding as casual as if mentioning she'd picked up milk at the store on her way home.

"Really? Wow, that was fast," I said, sitting up in the lounge chair.

"There was no reason to wait," she said. "And I've got a lot of work to do on it before you get down here next winter."

Just like that, the final decision about us making the move was made. I took a second to reflect on how I felt about it and decided, stingray love bite aside, that it sounded good. Then it immediately began to nag at me again.

"The house doesn't need that much work, Mom," I said, remembering the extensive tour we'd taken.

"Perhaps you're right. But just leave everything to me, darling."

"Can I ask what you paid for it?"

"About two million less than it's worth," she said.

"And that's all that really matters, right?" I said, parroting back one of her favorite real estate expressions.

"Well done, darling. You have been paying attention," she said, finally sitting down. "Now, what's with all this research you asked Gerald to do?"

"Oh, he told you, huh?"

"Of course, he told me. My daughter starts asking the Finance Minister, who just happens to be one of my closest friends, to look into corporate ownership and you didn't think he'd tell me?"

"In all honesty, I really didn't give it much thought, Mom," I said, frowning.

"And you think there's something there that is going to tell us who killed Wily and Crenshaw."

"Oh, I already know who killed them," I said, glancing over at her. "I'm just trying to get a better handle on the motives."

"I see. Are you going to tell me who it is?"

"No, I better wait until I get a chance to talk with Gerald."

"How about a hint?"

"Sure, why not?" I said, shrugging. "Okay, here's your hint. If you don't build it, maybe they won't come."

"That's it?" she said, frowning.

"It's all you need. At least as far as Crenshaw's murder is concerned."

"Have I ever told you that you have a tendency to lean toward the odd, darling?"

"Sure, all the time when I was a kid. It's something I got from you, right?"

"Highly unlikely," she said, smiling. "I knew I should have forced you to play with dolls when you were young."

"I did play with dolls."

"No, you didn't," she said, shaking her head. "You just used all the dolls I bought you as suspects in all those criminal line-ups you used to act out."

"I did, didn't I?" I said, smiling at the memory.

"And Barbie was the one that always got picked out of the lineup."

"Yeah, there was just something about her that always bothered me."

My mother laughed and reached over to give me a hug. I winced but returned it.

"You really are too much. You're convinced that the killer is going to be here tonight?"

"I'm positive, Mom."

"Don't you think we should be taking some precautions? I mean, if the killer is revealed tonight, aren't we going to be in danger?"

"No, the killer is pretty much done. There could be one more coming, but it won't happen here. But just to be safe, I invited that cute detective who has the hots for Chef Claire," I said, stretching back out in the lounge chair. "I told him to come prepared to make an arrest."

"Okay, darling, given your track record with these things, I'm going to trust you. But if you screw it up and embarrass me, I'm going to make sure you get the small bedroom."

"There's seven of them, Mom. I'm sure I'll find a place to sleep."

"Just be careful, okay?" she said, getting up. "I need to check in with Henry and make sure he's got everything he needs. You threw both of us a bit of a curveball with this last-minute dinner party."

"I noticed you managed to hit it," I said.

"Of course, darling. I always hit what you throw. What you need is a good change up."

"Yeah. I'm working on that, Mom."

A few minutes later, Gerald was the first guest to arrive, and he headed straight for me. He said hello to everyone then sat down next to me.

"How's your breast?" he said, giving me a coy smile.

"Word travels fast."

"Normally, we frown on tourists going topless down here, but I think we can make an exception for you," he said, trying not to laugh. "Given the rather unique circumstances and all that."

"Yeah, thanks, Gerald. I appreciate it," I said, making a face at him. "Do you have some news for me?"

"I do," he said, nodding. "And I have to say I'm impressed, Suzy. I have no idea how you put all of this together."

"It was all there. It just needed to be knitted together," I said. "So, how much did the company sell for?"

"Five hundred million."

"That's more than enough."

"It certainly is."

"And you found the local corporation down here behind the offer?" I said, sitting up and pulling my lounge chair closer to him.

"Eventually. As you know, down here corporate registrations tend to resemble a spider's web, especially when you're interested in not letting anybody know what you're up to."

"As was the case here, right?"

"Without a doubt. Do you really think that was enough of a reason to kill Crenshaw?"

"I do. It was a crime of passion."

Gerald gave me an odd look, and I continued.

"Not passion as it's usually defined. It was done by somebody with an intense passion for something they were worried about losing. Something bigger than themselves."

"But still..."

"And don't forget the plans the killer had. I'm sure an intense hatred developed when the deal went south," I said, then stared hard at him. "Were you the one who killed the deal, Gerald?"

"No, of course not," he said. "I didn't even know there was another offer on the table."

"Would you have tried to kill it if you had known?"

"That's a hard question to answer, Suzy."

"Not really."

Gerald took a beat to ponder my comment. "Yeah, I guess it's not," he said, shrugging. "Would I have tried to kill the other deal? Maybe. No, probably. Yeah, I probably would have."

"Because your job is to keep money moving and people building, right?"

"That's part of it. But Majestic Vista was simply too good of an opportunity to pass up."

"For you and your friends," I whispered.

"Yes. When you boil it down and strip away all the political rhetoric, it was a sweetheart deal for a very select few," he said, glancing over at me. "Is this the part where you turn sanctimonious?"

"No. I'm just sad."

"Odd choice. So, what's your take on the motive behind Wily's murder?"

"It was another crime of passion," I said. "But that passion had more of a…traditional nature to it."

"Love?"

"Jealousy."

"I see. Can I ask you why you invited Gloria to dinner?" Gerald said, shifting gears.

"I just thought she'd like the opportunity to confront her husband's killer," I said, forcing a smile.

"Gee, Suzy, why don't I believe you?"

"Force of habit, probably. But don't worry, Gerald. After tonight, I'm sure your job will be safe and sound."

"That would be great news. I love my job."

"Yes, I'm sure you do."

"So, is all this going to affect our friendship going forward?" he said.

"Not at all," I said, patting his hand. "It just clarifies it a bit."

"You lost me."

"Welcome to the club. I'm a bit lost myself. I'm in a bit of a quandary at the moment, Gerald. All these years, I've pretended that my mother's money didn't really have anything to do with me. But just today, she purchased a seven-bedroom beach house for us to live in."

"Oh, she got it," he said, perking up. "That's great."

"See, that's exactly what I'm talking about. How you just reacted to that bit of news. She bought the house from a couple that went belly up and had to get out in a hurry."

"That's the way the real estate market works sometimes. Somebody wins, somebody loses."

"No, that's the way *money* works, Gerald. This deal just happened to involve real estate. And now I'm no longer sitting on the sidelines as an observer, as someone who can make disparaging remarks about some of the things people with money do. Now, I've jumped in with both feet and given this lifestyle a big wet kiss."

"And lost the moral high ground?"

"No, I don't think that's it, although there have certainly been times in the past when I tried to take it. Now that I've willingly joined the club, so to speak, I'm worried about what it might do to me. I'm worried that some of my priorities are going to change."

"I wouldn't worry about it too much, Suzy. You seem pretty centered," he said. "And your mother does a good job handling it."

"Yeah, she does. But she lives in a completely different world from the one I'm used to. And I've always had the dogs to keep me focused on what's important."

"There's no reason for that to change."

"No, the dogs will always be my first priority. But now that I've said yes to her money, I'm concerned that I'm going to like it and will want to keep using it."

"I'm sure your mother has always spent money on you, right?"

"Oh, sure," I said, nodding. "Sometimes lavishly and way over the top. But it was always on birthday gifts or at Christmas. Then she helped us get the restaurant going, but that was an investment. That was different. The house is something else altogether. Or at least my complicity in it is."

"Complicity? That's a bit harsh, don't you think?"

"Gerald, right after we agreed to spend the winters down here, my mother walked into a real estate office today and wrote a check for nine million dollars."

"She got that place for nine million?" he said, stunned.

"See, that's what I'm talking about," I said, my voice rising.

"What?"

"You're surprised by how good a deal she got, and not the ridiculous fact that she was able to write a check that size right on the spot. Who does that?"

"Probably more people than you think," he said, shrugging.

"She just took her checkbook out, wrote down all those zeroes, and handed it over."

"Well, she sure couldn't be lugging around nine million in cash," he said, laughing.

"Money," I said, shaking my head. "It's such an incredibly powerful engine to have at your disposal. It's like a giant steamroller crushing everything it comes in contact with."

"And you're worried that you're going to get run over?"

"No, I'm starting to worry that I'm gonna want to drive."

Chapter 29

The other guests started arriving around six and were soon sitting around the pool area with fresh cocktails. Timothy, the boring financial consultant, arrived first, and he made a beeline for me. But I was able to quickly pawn him off on Josie, and I made my escape. She glared at me, and I gave her a smile and a taunting finger wave as I headed for the barbecue area.

Thomas and Sally arrived shortly after, followed by Prunella, Wily's widow, then Sky. He was wearing a hand-painted sling around his injured shoulder, and I watched him carefully as he and Sally kept sneaking longing glances at each other. Her husband, Thomas, was either oblivious or indifferent, and he spent his first half-hour chatting with Gerald.

Bill and Jerry kept pounding Mudslides, and I wondered if they could keep up their current pace without passing out before dinner. Bill seemed to be holding his own, but Jerry slumped a bit lower in her chair after each drink. On my way into the house to grab a few more bottles of champagne, I stopped in front of them.

"How are you guys doing?" I said.

"We're great," Bill said. "I always love this time of day. And the Mudslides sure are going down easy."

"Drink all you want," I said. "We'll make more."

"You stole that line," he said, grinning as he tried to remember where he'd heard it. "A doughnut commercial, right?"

"You caught me."

"How's your boobie?" Jerry said, trying to focus.

"It's really sore," I said.

"Don't worry about it," she said, waving it off. "I've had much worse."

"Yes, I'm sure you have," I said.

She frowned up at me, then glanced at her husband.

"Maybe you should slow down a bit, dear," he said, reaching for her glass.

She swatted his hand away, drained what was left in the glass, then headed for the drink table.

"Don't mind her," Bill said. "She has a hard time saying no to Mudslides."

"Don't worry about it. It's a party, right?"

"Exactly," he said, raising his glass to me.

I gave him a small wave and headed for the kitchen. On my way in, Prunella was coming out of the bathroom and startled me.

"Oh, I didn't see you coming," I said. "How are you doing?"

"I fine," she said with a tired voice. "I'm still adjusting to not having him around."

"I can only imagine. How long were you and Wily married?"

"Too long," she said, then headed back outside.

"Okay, then," I said to myself as I rummaged through one of the fridges.

I grabbed four bottles of champagne, headed outside, and placed them in ice buckets. I glanced around looking for something else to do, then noticed Gloria Crenshaw making her way across the lawn. She was dressed in what my mother liked to call *elegant casual*, and wearing shorts and a matching top that highlighted her tan. I considered walking across the lawn to greet her, but decided to wait and watch the expressions when the other guests realized she was there.

Bill and Jerry were the first to notice, and they stared at her in disbelief like she was either walking on water or had appeared as some sort of ghostly vision. Gerald and Thomas studied her closely as she got closer, and the rest of the guests seemed to have a mixture of shock and anger on their faces. Gloria just kept strolling across the lawn with a small fixed smile, casually glancing around at the house and landscaping. My mother finally noticed her presence and headed over to greet her. I followed my mother, and all of three of us met at the same time on the edge of the pool.

"I'm so glad you could make it, Gloria," my mother said, giving her a quick hug.

"Thanks. I just couldn't pass up your daughter's invitation," she said, giving me a coy smile.

"She can be very persuasive," my mother said.

"I get that from you, Mom."

"Yes, and I always thought it was one of your better qualities, darling. Now, why don't you go get Gloria a glass of champagne?"

Fastball. Right down the middle. I never saw it coming.

"I'll go with you," Gloria said, following me.

As we strolled across the lawn, she put her hand on my arm and stopped walking.

"How are you planning on handling this?"

"Well, I thought we'd eat first," I said. "No sense ruining our appetite, right?"

"Or trying to confront my husband's killer on an empty stomach?" she said, casually.

"Exactly. I don't know if it's just my imagination, but you seem different tonight."

"That's because I haven't had a drink all day," she said. "I wanted to be sober for this conversation."

"Sure, I get that. You want your message to be loud and clear, right?"

"Actually, I just wanted to make sure I'd be able to remember it later."

Chapter 30

In addition to providing delicious nourishment, the magnificent feast my mother had put together on short notice also served another valuable function: It enabled everyone around the table to focus on eating thereby giving them an excuse for not talking to each other. Gloria's presence definitely had everyone off balance, and the guests shared confused looks with each other when they sat down to eat. They kept sneaking glances at her all throughout dinner. If Gloria was bothered by or even noticed the furtive attention, she did a good job hiding it, and she ate quietly chatting with my mother and me.

"Could you pass the rice, please?" Josie said.

I stretched forward then handed her the bowl.

"I would have thought you'd be more interested in the calamari," I said.

"No, not tonight," she said, shaking her head as she spooned a generous serving of the pilaf onto her plate. "After today, I think it's gonna be awhile. And I'm very happy there's no grilled stingray in sight."

"Don't start."

"Because that would really *suck*, you know?" she deadpanned before taking a bite of lobster.

I heard Chef Claire snort, and I leaned forward and looked down the table.

"Don't encourage her," I said, then settled back into my seat. "Are there any sparks between those two?"

"Well, he looks like he's about to burst," Josie said, glancing over at the detective. "But she isn't interested at all. By the way, when I asked Chef Claire what he was doing here, she said she was just doing you a favor. Are you expecting to need his help tonight?"

"I don't think so," I said. "But we'll see how things go."

"Suzy?"

"Yeah."

"What are you up to?"

"Nothing. What's the detective's name again?"

"Detective Renfro."

"Right," I said, nodding as I glanced around the table. "Okay, it looks like everyone is done eating. It's Showtime."

"I haven't had dessert yet."

"Suck it up."

I stood up and tapped my water glass with a spoon. Everyone fell quiet and looked at me. I cleared my throat and took a sip of champagne.

"I'd just like to say thank you to everyone for taking the time to come by tonight to say goodbye. All three of us have had…let's say, a very interesting week down here."

A round of soft laughter and nervous chuckles broke out then faded.

"And since our first night here ended in tragedy, we thought that we would try again to see if we could have more of a normal dinner party."

"Normal?" Thomas blurted as he glared at Gloria. "That's going to be a bit difficult with the Evil Queen here, wouldn't you say?"

"Thomas!" my mother said, her eyes flaring. "You will not speak to one of my guests like that."

"I wasn't talking to her, I was talking about her," he said, trying to match my mother's glare. Then he quickly backed down and held up his hands. "I'm sorry. But that woman is going to do everything she can to put all of us out of business."

"This is not the place, Thomas," Gerald said.

"Oh, shut up, Gerald," Thomas said. "If it wasn't for you, we might never have gotten into this predicament in the first place."

"Yeah, I really had to twist your arm, didn't I, Thomas?" Gerald said.

"You and your *we're gonna make millions*," Thomas said, shaking his head.

"Thomas, please," Sally said, placing a hand over his.

"Stay out of this, Sally. In fact, why don't you and your boy-toy go take a long walk on the beach and leave the conversation to the adults?"

Sally flinched and gave Sky a quick look but stayed silent. Her husband stared at her then continued.

"Well, if you're going to stay, at least keep your mouth shut. Yeah, that's it, go ahead and cry. Maybe Sherwin Williams over there will let you wipe your eyes on his sling."

"What a pig," Josie whispered.

"At least you were actually invited to participate, Thomas," Timothy said. "I did most of the analysis, and all I got was the opportunity to get coffee and make copies."

"Oh, stop whining," Thomas said. "You got paid, didn't you?"

"I should have been invited in, and you know it," Timothy whispered.

"It's all irrelevant now, Timothy," Thomas said. "It's ancient history. Isn't that right, Gloria?"

"You're disgusting," Gloria said.

"Can I get an amen?" Sally said.

"Well, I must say this is going very well," my mother said, leaning behind Gloria's chair to talk to me. "Is this what you had in mind, darling?"

"Just give it a minute, Mom."

"Oh, good, there's more."

"I'm sorry, Gloria," Bill said, speaking carefully so he wouldn't slur his words. "But I need to ask. Why are you here?"

"Suzy invited me," she said.

"Why would you do that?" Bill said, speaking to me but looking at Gloria.

"I'm over here, Bill," I said, giving him a small wave. "I believe Gloria has something to tell you, and this seemed like the perfect place to do it."

"Oh. Okay," Bill said, somewhat confused but mollified for the moment. "What do you have to tell us?"

All eyes settled on Gloria, and she took her time getting ready to speak. She finished her glass of champagne, wiped her mouth with her napkin, then tossed it on the table.

"I've given the matter a great deal of thought, and I've made a decision."

"Here it comes," Thomas said, sighing. "It's been nice knowing all of you."

"Don't be so dramatic," Gerald said.

"That's easy for you to say. You don't have every nickel to your name plus a big bank loan tied up in this thing."

"I warned you about getting too greedy," Gerald said. "Go ahead, Gloria,"

"Yes, too greedy. That pretty much sums it up, doesn't it? I've decided to make some major changes in my life. And one of those changes is to leave the Caymans. I'm selling the house and moving, me and all my money, elsewhere. I need a fresh start. To be perfectly honest, most of you creep me out, and I want to get as far away from you as I possibly can. As such, I've instructed my lawyers to drop the injunction. And as soon as I get my hundred million back, you'll be free and clear to find some other investors and do whatever deal you want."

I wasn't sure if Gloria had actually made up her to leave the island, or if she was merely playing the part we'd discussed in her sunroom. But it sure sounded like she was telling the truth, and I leaned forward on my elbows and waited for everyone's reaction.

Gerald emitted a contented sigh I assumed was the sound of newfound job security. Thomas made a yipping sound that reminded me of a noise Chloe made when she was very happy with a dog treat I'd given her. Everyone else, at least those who had a stake in Majestic Vista, smiled at each other then gave Gloria a golf clap. Obviously annoyed by the scene, she waited it out with a blank stare, then sat back in her chair. I took a sip of champagne and continued to gauge the reactions. Josie leaned over closer.

"I feel like I'm missing something," she whispered. "Or was this your whole plan?"

I nodded my head at Bill who was giving Gloria a very dark look. Josie snuck a quick glance at him, then gave me a wild-eyed stare.

"No way," she whispered.

"Yeah," I said.

"Really?"

"Yeah, I'm positive. It's sad, huh?"

"I don't believe it."

"Just give it a minute," I said, then leaned forward. "Are you okay, Bill?"

"What?" he said, glancing around until he connected my face to the voice. "Yeah, I'm fine." He turned to Gloria. "Why would you do something like that?"

"I decided that life's just too short," she said, giving me a quick smile.

"But this is your chance to…"

"Her chance to do what, Bill?" Gerald said.

"I'm not talking to you. But I must say that you seem pleased by the news," Bill said, draining the last half of his Mudslides.

"How many of those has he had?" Josie whispered.

"Let's just say it's a good thing he's barefoot because he'll need his toes to help him count," I said.

"That's your strategy?" she said. "Get a confession out of him while he's hammered?"

"I was just hoping to back him into a corner. He came up with the hammered part all on his own."

"I don't know," Josie said, frowning. "It doesn't seem fair."

"Fair? He killed two people."

"Maybe," Josie said, then caught the glare I was giving her. "Look, I'm not saying he didn't do it, but this doesn't have your usual flair. The booze seems to cheapen it. Like it's giving you an unfair advantage."

"Everybody's a critic," I said, then refocused on Bill who seemed to be concentrating hard.

"I can't believe it," he finally said. "You had them."

"Had who, Bill?" Thomas said as he pushed his plate away.

"You. All of you," Bill said, looking around but not managing to make eye contact with anyone at the table. "I can't believe you're going to let them off the hook."

"I just don't have the energy for it," Gloria said, shrugging. "All I want to do is find out who killed Jerome, then get out of here."

"But you could have tied them up in court for years," Bill said. "You could have wiped Thomas completely out, not to mention this government lackey posing as a man of the people."

"How dare you speak to me like that," Gerald said.

"Oh, shut it, Gerald," Bill said. "You're a corrupt, bottom feeding political hack with both hands out. And don't give me that wounded look. Trust me, everybody knows."

My mother reached out and squeezed Gerald's hand. Gerald looked at her, and she slowly shook her head as they held each other's eyes. Gerald sat back in his seat and folded his arms across his chest.

"You're making a huge mistake, Gloria," Bill said. "This was your big chance to do the right thing."

"This is my chance to get the hell out of here," Gloria said. "And I'm taking it."

"What a waste," Bill said with an exhausted sigh.

"Well, look on the bright side, Bill," I said, way too chirpy. "Now, you'll have another chance to try and put your own deal together."

Bill and Jerry flushed red with embarrassment, although I'm sure the Mudslides helped add some of the color. The others, including my mother and Gloria, looked at the couple then their eyes settled on me.

"Do you want to explain it, Bill? Or would you like me to go first?"

"I have no idea what you're talking about," he said, slurring his words.

"Okay, then let me give it a shot," I said. "Several months ago, a holding company with a bunch of subsidiaries buried inside it made an offer on a certain piece of property. But before the owner could decide whether or not he was going to accept the offer, the investor group led by Jerome Crenshaw swooped in with their plans for Majestic Vista and snatched the property up. And that was the end of whatever plans the holding company had for the property."

"Fascinating story, Suzy," Bill said. "But what does that have to do with me?"

"The holding company and most of the subsidiaries all belong to you," I said, shrugging.

"Is that right? Now I'm the owner of a web of shadow companies? You're out of your mind," he said, laughing. Then he frowned. "Am I supposed to believe that you figured all this out by yourself?"

"No, Gerald did."

"What?" Bill said, glaring at Gerald. "You've been spying on me?"

"Hey, I'm just a corrupt bottom feeder, so it took me a few days. But it was all there," Gerald said. "You just have to know where to look."

"And having an interest in actually finding out the facts also helps, right, Gerald?" I said.

He gave me a dirty look but chose not to comment.

"So, Jerry and I have some financial interests we like to keep quiet. Who down here doesn't?"

The others around the table had to concede the point and nodded.

"I'm sorry, darling, but is there a point to all this?"

"The point is that Bill was extremely upset when his offer was turned down, and Jerome's group was selected."

"No one likes getting beat out of a great deal, darling. That shouldn't surprise you."

"You're right, Mom. But this one was different. While Bill was mad about losing the deal, it was the idea of how the land was going to be used that enraged him."

"I'm not going to sit here and listen to this," Bill said. "Collect your things, Jerry. We're out of here."

"Not quite yet, sir," Detective Renfro said. "Please, just have a seat. Let's see how the conversation goes from here."

"I can't believe this," Bill said, glaring at me. "And to think we were nice enough to take you out to feed the stingrays."

"Probably not the strongest argument you could use, Bill," Josie said.

"Don't start," I said, suppressing a giggle.

"What were your plans for the property, Bill?" my mother said.

"Ask her," Bill said, pointing at me. "She's the one who thinks she's got all the answers."

"Okay," my mother said. "Darling, would you mind explaining?"

"They planned on buying the property and just sitting on it. Then at some point, I imagine they hoped they'd be able to get the government to designate it as a protected area."

"You two are a couple of closeted environmentalists?" Thomas said. "I knew there was a reason I didn't like you."

"Yes, they are. And I have no idea why they felt the need to keep it quiet. But they must have had a lot of wonderful plans for spending all the money they made when Bill's company was sold." I smiled at the couple, then felt a wave of sadness wash over me for what was about to happen to them.

"And once I was able to figure out your corporate structure," Gerald said. "I did some additional digging and was able to connect the dots on some rather generous and anonymous contributions to environmental and conservation groups."

"So, Jerry and I are interested in what happens to the planet, especially in our own backyard. What's wrong with that?"

"Commie," Thomas snapped.

"The property where Majestic Vista was supposed to be built is apparently home to several endangered species. Plants and trees. As well as some parrots and the Blue Iguana."

"And the Boobies," Jerry said.

"What?" I said, staring at her.

"Oh, not yours," she said, waving the idea off. "Booby the bird. The Red-footed Booby."

"Well, her's is pretty red at the moment," Josie said.

"Shut it."

"And if you have any more situations like the one we had today, we might have to put yours on the endangered list," Josie deadpanned, then flinched. "Ow. That hurt."

"It's supposed to hurt," I said. "Knock it off."

Gloria waited out our back and forth then looked over at me with a pained expression.

"Are you saying he killed Jerome because he was upset about further development on the islands?"

"Yes, Majestic Vista, while a magnificent development project, runs contrary to everything Bill and Jerry want to happen down here. I hate saying it, but that's exactly what happened."

"This is ridiculous," Bill said, about to get up out of his chair but deciding against it when he saw the look Detective Renfro was giving him.

"On the night your husband was killed, I noticed Bill and Jerry leave the party and head for the beach. Then just a few minutes later, I saw Jerry chatting with Sky at the bar."

"I told you to stay on the beach," Bill whispered.

"I was bored," Jerry said.

"I knew it," Sally said, glaring at Sky. "I knew you two had been sneaking off behind my back."

"Sally, please," Sky said. "Let's not do this here."

I waited for the table to quiet down before continuing.

"And after Jerome collapsed on the verandah, Gerald and some other men were doing what they could to help him. Then all of a sudden, I noticed Bill standing at the back of the group."

"So what?" Bill said. "I was just trying to do my part. To see if there was anything I could do."

"Yes, but you just appeared out of thin air. I was watching very closely, and there was no way you walked across the lawn and then up onto the verandah. And the only way you would have been able to join the rest of the group was by coming out of the house."

"Maybe I had to use the bathroom," Bill said, chugging from a bottle of water, trying to sober up in a hurry.

"Maybe," I said, nodding. "But I saw your reaction earlier when Jerome tackled Gloria on the beach. He was very rough with her, and that seemed to trigger something in you. Your rage about how he was manhandling Gloria was impossible to miss."

Bill and Jerry both flinched, and I looked over when I heard Gloria sigh.

"That wasn't one of my finest moments," she said.

"No, but your husband had no right to treat you that way. Did he, Bill?"

"No man has a right to do that to any woman."

"You'll get no argument from me. But I imagine that sort of thing went on all the time at those parties," I said, deciding to push the envelope.

"It did. I hated those parties," Gloria said.

"Yes, so you said. And I imagine Bill felt the same way you did about them."

"They were disgusting," Bill said, glancing at Jerry.

"But if you wanted to play in the big leagues down here with the money people, you felt you had to go along with them, right? Just to prove you were one of the guys and worthy of being included in all the important conversations."

"I have no idea what you're talking about," he whispered.

"But then Jerry decided she liked the parties," I said, studying her face. "And she liked them a lot. Right, Jerry?"

"Please, stop. What does that have to do with anything?"

"Well, for one, after you started hooking up with Wily outside of the parties, it gave Bill a motive to kill him."

"That's ridiculous," Jerry said, laughing as she glanced at her husband. Then her face fell when she saw the look on his face. "Tell her, Bill. Tell her how crazy that idea is."

"They were definitely getting together regularly," Prunella said. "Wily told me you two were quite the item."

"What?" Jerry said, staring at Prunella. "Why would he tell you that?"

"To throw it in my face, primarily. That's the way Wily was. You would have figured it out, eventually."

"You couldn't miss it. He wouldn't leave you alone," Bill said. "Even after I told him in no uncertain terms to knock it off."

"You killed Wily?" Jerry whispered.

Maybe he was simply tired of carrying it around, or maybe it was all the Mudslides he'd knocked back. It was probably a lot of both I decided when Bill looked around the table, rubbed his forehead, and then slowly nodded.

"Yeah."

"Why on earth would you do something like that? I mean, Crenshaw, sure, I get killing him. He was the one who was going to wipe out our dream. But Wily? How could you do that?"

"Actually, it was pretty easy," Bill said, suddenly, inexplicably chatty. "We were sitting on the couch next to Chef Claire talking, and he kept staring at you like you were a piece of meat. And I flashed back to one of those parties when he'd given you the same look. I'd just finished eating, and I was playing with one of the metal skewers. I started fantasizing about how much I'd love to stab him in the chest with it and watch him die a slow, painful death. Then the lights went out, and I just went for it. I was back on the couch before you even knew I'd left."

"I can't believe it," Jerry said, tearing up.

"The only thing I felt bad about was the fact that it was too dark to watch him bleed out."

Then Bill looked around the table as if he'd forgotten all of us were sitting there listening to him and his wife talk. I decided to go for broke and leaned forward to speak directly to Bill.

"And then the other day when we were diving, you saw Sky drop the spear gun, and you grabbed it and took your shot. It didn't discharge by itself, did it, Bill? It wasn't an accident."

"How on earth did you figure that out?" he said, his eyes wide. "I mean, that's crazy."

"You shot me in the shoulder on purpose?" Sky said.

"No, that was a mistake. Believe me, that's not what I was aiming for."

"Why would you do that?" Sky said.

"Because you're sleeping with my wife, you moron," Bill said.

"I'm also sleeping with his wife," Sky said, pointing at Thomas. "But you don't see him taking potshots at me."

"Just be patient. It won't be long," Thomas said to Sky, then remembered that Detective Renfro was sitting at the table. "Not that I'd ever do something crazy like that, of course."

Jerry stared at her husband is disbelief.

"What happened to you?" she whispered.

"Funny, dear. I was planning on asking you the same question."

Detective Renfro stood and kept a close eye on both Bill and Jerry as he walked around the table to handcuff them. He made a call, thanked all of us for our hospitality, then escorted both of them across the lawn and into his car. We watched him drive away, and then some of the other guests quickly packed up and left. Gerald said his goodbyes to my mother then headed toward me.

"I guess I should thank you," he said, giving me a hug I only half-returned.

"What are you thanking me for, Gerald?"

"Well, for bailing me out of a major jam for one," he said. "And, of course, for solving both murders."

"In that order, right?"

"What do you want me to say, Suzy? That I was scared to death I was going to lose my job?"

"Say anything you want, Gerald. I was just checking on your priorities."

"Okay, I get it," he said, nodding. "I guess we're going to need some time before you let me off the hook."

"Yeah, I think we will," I said, nodding. "You take care of yourself."

"You too. I'll see you soon. Maybe I'll get an invitation to the housewarming party," he said, grinning at me.

"I'm sure you'll be invited, Gerald," I said, nodding at my mother.

"She's a good one to have in your corner. You be good now."

"You too, Gerald. Try to stay out of trouble."

"Where's the fun in that?"

I watched him head for his car, then glanced around to see who was left. Prunella was still sitting at the dinner table staring up at the night sky. Gloria had sat down in one of the lounge chairs around the pool. Josie was headed for the garage, and soon I noticed Bailey along with mama and the puppies make a mad dash for the pool. Soon, all eight were in the pool and fighting over the tennis balls Josie had tossed in. Initially worried about Gloria's reaction to the dogs, I looked over and saw a huge smile on her face as she watched them. I thought about what she'd been through the past few days, and decided it was probably the most genuine smile she'd been able to summon up in some time. I waved at Prunella, and she slowly made her way across the lawn to join us. My mother stretched out in one of the lounge chairs and glanced around at the group.

"It looks like it's just us girls," she said.

"It's about time," Chef Claire said. "Between the fawning detective who wants to have a half dozen kids and that boring guy on the other side of me during dinner, I was about to lose it. What was his name again?"

"Timothy," Josie said.

"I thought you said he was really interesting to talk to," Chef Claire said.

"You must have misheard me," Josie deadpanned.

"I can't believe Bill was the one who killed Wily," Prunella said to the night air.

"Are you going to be okay?" my mother said.

"I'll be fine," she said, reaching down to play with one of the puppies. "Wily and my days together were already numbered. I just never expected them to end the way they did."

"I'm so sorry you have to go through this," my mother said.

"Don't worry about it," Prunella said, shaking her head. "Gradually, I stopped caring what Wily did. And, eventually, I stopped even noticing."

"I guess this is the part where people always offer their condolences by saying that he's in a better place now," my mother said.

"As long as there are booze and women where he ended up, probably," Prunella said, then she lost her battle not to laugh.

We watched her as the laugh played out, then she sighed and fell silent. Then she glanced around at us.

"I'm sorry," she said. "I probably shouldn't have laughed at that. But I just couldn't help it."

"I thought it was funny," Josie said. "But I wasn't going to be the first one to laugh. Suzy has already yelled at me enough for one day."

"Do whatever you want," I said, shrugging. "I'm too tired to worry about it."

"You did good, Snoopmeister," Josie said.

"Yes, darling. It was a very impressive performance. I still can't believe those two would do something like that."

"It was the way they always talked about nature that first got me thinking," I said. "And when Gerald said they passed on Majestic Vista, I wondered why anybody would pass up what sounds like a sure thing. You know, easy money and all that."

"I thought I picked up on something when we were on the boat," Chef Claire said. "The way they looked at their surroundings and the way they were always talking about Mother Nature. It was…reverential."

"Oh, good word," Josie said.

"As soon as I made the environmental connection, I was pretty sure I was on the right track," I said. "Then I noticed the way Sky and Jerry looked at each other on the boat. Bill noticed as well. He was not a happy man."

"But how did you know Bill was the one who shot Sky?" Chef Claire said. "I almost fell out of my chair when you got that one right."

"That was just a lucky guess," I said, shrugging. "I figured that since I was on a roll, I'd just go for it. He'd already confessed to killing Wily and Jerome, so I decided it couldn't hurt to ask. No harm, no foul, right?"

"I guess all those years playing with Barbie came in handy," my mother said, shaking her head.

"What are you babbling about, Mrs. C.?" Josie said.

"Nothing, dear. Just a little trip down memory lane," my mother said, winking at me.

"They're both going away for a very long time, aren't they?" Gloria said.

"Him, definitely," I said. "If she gets the right lawyer, Jerry might do okay since she didn't actually kill either one."

"She's still an accessory," Josie said.

"Yeah, she is. It's hard to say what they'll do to Jerry," I said. "What do you think, Gloria?"

"I think I'd like a cold drink. Something with a whole bunch of alcohol in it."

"Then you have come to the right place," I said, standing up. "Mudslides for all."

"Just don't have too many," my mother said. "Unless chatty is what you're going for. Poor Bill. He just didn't know when to shut up."

"I just remembered something really important," Josie said.

"What's that?" I said, frowning.

"We didn't have dessert."

"Put some ice cream in your mudslide."

"It's not the same," Josie said.

"Well, I'm sorry. You're just going to have to deal with it."

"There's a tray of brownies in the kitchen."

"Then go get them. You've got two legs."

"I'm exhausted," she said, yawning. "I spent all afternoon rescuing you from the clutches of that stingray."

"Don't start."

"But I was happy to do it. All of us need to do everything we can to protect endangered species."

"It's not endangered," I snapped. "Just a little bruised and chafed."

"Tomato, tomahto."

Gloria's head swiveled back and forth as she listened to us squabble. Then she looked at my mother.

"Are they always like this?"

"This?" my mother said, yawning. "This is nothing."

Chapter 31

I walked around the dining room then poked my head inside the kitchen. Then I sat down next to Josie at the bar and swiveled back and forth on my stool. Chef Claire was standing a few feet away waiting to hear our reaction.

"I like it," I said. "But you're the one who needs to be happy. What do you think?"

"I think it'll work," Chef Claire said. "It's been out of business for a couple of years, so we'll need to replace a lot of the furnishings. And the kitchen needs a bit of an upgrade. But it's got good bones, and I like the layout."

"And it needs to be painted," Josie said. "Lime green? What were they thinking?"

"I know. And that color conjures up a really bad memory," I said.

"I thought we agreed never to speak of that again," Josie said, frowning.

"Sorry."

"How much can we spend on it?" Chef Claire said.

"Whatever it takes," I said, glancing up at the overhead lighting.

"Just like that?" Chef Claire said.

"Yeah. Just like that."

"I gotta say, Suzy," Chef Claire said. "You're kind of freaking me out here."

"Why's that?"

"Your new cavalier approach to spending money," Chef Claire said.

"It's not cavalier," I said. "If you say it's a good investment and that we can make money with a restaurant down here, I'm going to trust you."

"And we've had your food, remember?" Josie said.

"Exactly," I said, smiling. "What sort of menu are you thinking about?"

"Primarily seafood."

"Yuk," I said, frowning.

"Perfect," Josie said. "I've been thinking about switching to a seafood diet for at least part of the year."

"Yeah, your seafood diet. You see food, and you eat it."

"Funny."

"Suzy, we're in the Cayman Islands surrounded by the ocean. The menu has to emphasize seafood," Chef Claire said. "But I'll make sure there are enough choices for you. Don't worry, you won't starve. I'm thinking about going with traditional Caribbean fused with Asian and Indian."

"Interesting," I said, nodding as I took another look around the dining room. "Okay, I vote yes. What about you guys?"

They looked at each other and nodded, and we placed our hands together to seal the deal.

"I'm going to have to spend some time down here over the next few months," Chef Claire said. "I've got a million things to do."

"You poor baby," Josie said, laughing.

Then we all looked at the front door when we heard the soft knock. Teresa Williams was standing in the doorway with a confused look on her face. Then she waved to us after her eyes adjusted to the light.

"I'm in the right place after all," she said, walking toward us. "I wasn't sure when I saw it from the outside. It looks abandoned."

"Yeah, it needs a bit of work, doesn't it?" Chef Claire said.

"And hopefully a paint job," she said, glancing around. "That lime green is enough to give you nightmares."

"Teresa, you have no idea," Josie said. "Thanks for coming over. We're on our way to the airport and thought we'd kill two birds with one stone."

"No problem," she said. "But I do have to ask, this is where you plan to put the animal shelter?"

"No," I said. "This is going to be a restaurant."

"You're opening an animal shelter and a restaurant?" she said.

"Now, there's an idea," Josie said. "We could combine the two and call it…Eat and Fetch. Or maybe, The Barking Belly."

"What?" Teresa said, thoroughly confused.

"Don't worry," I said. "You'll eventually get used to her. It's sort of like learning to live with high blood pressure. The animal shelter is going to be built not far from here."

"You're going to build from scratch?" Teresa said.

"Yes," I said.

"And you want me to run it?"

"Absolutely."

"Why?"

"Because it looks like it's something the place needs," Josie said. "And you obviously love animals as much as we do."

"And we're only going to be down here during the winter," I said. "So, we're going to need someone to take care of the place."

"I have so many questions," she said.

"And we'll be more than happy to answer all of them, Teresa," Josie said. "But all we need to know at the moment is if you're interested. We'll need someone on the ground to work with the architect and then the construction crew."

"Yes, of course, I'm interested," she said. "But you do know that there isn't a lot of money to be made taking care of animals, don't you?"

"We do okay," I said, glancing at Josie who nodded. "And don't worry about money."

"I'm a single mother with two daughters," she said. "I always worry about money."

"Well, we'll see what we can do about that," I said, glancing at my watch. "Look, we really need to get to the airport. My mother does not like to be kept waiting. We'll give you a call in a couple of days after we get home, and we'll start sorting out all the details."

We all gave her a hug and left her standing by her car puzzled but happy. I drove with Chef Claire sitting in the passenger seat and Josie sprawled across the backseat.

"She seems very nice," Chef Claire said.

"Yes, she does," I said, focusing on the road. "And her daughters seem to be really good kids."

"She's going to do great," Josie said. "Hey, haven't you learned anything from your mother this week? Slow down. I'm trying to savor these last few minutes."

"Don't remind me," Chef Claire said. "I checked the weather back home this morning."

"And?" I said, glancing over.

"Seven degrees. Warming to a high of twenty with a chance of snow."

"Perfect," Josie said. "My tan will be gone in a week. Hey, I almost forgot to ask. How's your love bite?"

"Why don't we just leave her here?" I said to Chef Claire.

"Don't even think about it," Josie said. "I need to get home to see my beautiful boy."

I smiled as I pulled into the airport. The thought of seeing Chloe and the rest of our dogs made the prospect of enduring several more weeks of winter almost sound appealing. I parked next to my mother, grabbed the keys from the ignition, and tossed them to Henry who was standing next to her.

"You're late," my mother said, bussing my cheek. "How did it go?"

"We're taking the restaurant, and Teresa is interested in running the shelter," I said.

"Wonderful," she said, softly clapping her hands. "There's no backing out now."

"Yeah, you win, Mom," I said, laughing.

"We all won, darling," she said, glancing at a panel van that was pulling into the airport. "There he is." She walked over to the van and spoke with the driver. He nodded, then drove toward the back of the airport.

"Okay," my mother said. "The dogs are all here safe and sound and headed for the plane. Let's go. Your chariot awaits."

Henry tossed the car keys back to me, and my mother hopped into the passenger seat and gestured for Henry to follow the van. We did the same and moments later we parked on the tarmac next to a luxury jet that looked more suited for a rock star than the three of us with eight dogs in tow. We climbed out of the jeep and stared at the plane.

"You do know that this flight is going to spoil us forever, don't you?" Josie said.

"Yeah," I said, unable to take my eyes off the plane.

"Are you going to be okay with that?"

"I think I'll manage."

"Good, because if you couldn't, I'd be forced to have you committed and then find a new friend."

"Okay, ladies," my mother said. "Look sharp. Here comes immigration. Make sure you have your passports and all the dogs' documentation ready."

"Well, look who it is," the man from immigration said, giving my mother a long hug.

"Julio, it's so good to see you," she said. "I had no idea you were working today."

"Yeah, right," he said, laughing. "And this must be your daughter. The resemblance is incredible."

"Thank you. I've been trying to tell her that for years," my mother said, grinning as she looked at me. "Go ahead, Julio. Tell her how lucky she is."

"Ah, geez, Mom."

"Schoolgirl alert," Josie said.

"Shut it."

"Okay," the immigration man said, studying our passports. "These look fine. And I believe we have some dogs making the trip with you. Two adults and four puppies."

"No, that's incorrect," I said. "There's actually six puppies."

"Not according to this docket," he said. "I'm sorry, but it says four."

"Oh, no. What the heck happened with the paperwork?" I said, looking at Josie.

"It said six when I saw it," she said.

"No, darling, Julio is correct. It's four."

"Mom? Please explain," I said, fighting back a rush of panic.

"Relax. The other two are just fine."

"But they're not here?"

"No, they're back at the house resting comfortably," she said, grinning at Henry. "We were talking last night, and we decided that having a couple companions around the place was a great idea."

"You? You plan to adopt two of the puppies?" I said, baffled.

"Oh, there's no need for a plan. I already did it."

"Which puppies did you take?" Josie said, also thoroughly confused by my mother's abrupt change of position about owning a dog.

"You know the two who are inseparable and are always off playing by themselves?"

"You're taking both of them?" I said.

"Well, I couldn't do something silly and split them up, could I?"

"Unbelievable," I said. "I'm speechless."

"Well, that's a first. I guess miracles do happen," my mother said. "You don't mind, do you?"

"No, Mom. I don't mind at all. You do know what you're getting into, right?"

"After watching the two of you all these years, yes, I think I have a very clear idea."

A soft okay and a hug was all I could manage.

"You're all set," the immigration man said. "It was so good to see you, Mrs. C."

"You too, Julio. Say hello to the family for me. And we must get together soon."

He waved goodbye and strolled back toward the terminal. We watched the driver of the van carry the dog cages up the stairs onto the plane.

"That's your cue," my mother said. "Call me as soon as you land."

"Will do, Mom," I said, giving her another hug. "Say, have you given any thought to what you're going to name the dogs?"

"Summer and Winter," she said, smiling at Henry.

"Catchy," Josie said. "I like it."

"I thought it had sort of a Zen quality to it," my mother said.

"Yeah, you'll have to explain that to me sometime, Mom. Okay, let's do this."

We said our goodbyes and headed up the stairs onto the plane. Both Chef Claire and Josie made it a point not to sit next to me, and I glanced over at them.

"What is it? Are you worried I didn't shower this morning?"

"No, let's just say we're taking precautions in case we hit any turbulence," Josie said.

"Fine. More room for the dogs," I said, glancing around the plane. "This is nice."

"Suzy, this plane would have to crash into the ocean before it could be called just nice," Chef Claire said.

"Good point," I said, gripping my armrests hard as the plane roared down the runway then climbed.

When the plane leveled off, we unfastened our seatbelts and headed for the cages that were secured to the seats. We opened them and were greeted by the sad, soulful expressions of six pairs of eyes. I laughed and knelt down and rubbed their heads before standing.

"Are you guys ready to come out and play?"

Epilogue

The memories of eighty-degree temperatures and white sand faded and were soon replaced by bone-chilling cold and a different white substance that had continued to fall since we'd landed. Things around the Inn had continued without a hitch, and Sammy and Jill had done a great job running things as well as housesitting. We spent our first night back around the fireplace playing with the dogs and making sure they were comfortable with each other. The puppies weren't quite sure what to make of this thing called snow, and they spent most of their first five minutes outside trying to snatch snowflakes out of the air.

The next morning, we made the walk from the house down to the Inn, and, by lunchtime, it was like we'd never been away. And after nine successive days of constant snow and cold, even though it was great to be home, I was more than ready for an extended bout of tropical heat and a cold Mudslide.

On a cold, snowy Sunday morning, Josie and I stared out the picture window next to the reception desk and watched Jackson plow the two-acre play area. The snowbanks were fifteen feet high in a couple of areas and growing by the day. Most of the dogs had gotten increasingly efficient and cut their time outside down to the absolute minimum required to take care of business. Except for Captain and Chloe. They loved rolling around in the snow and had been encouraging their new housemate, Bailey, to join them. But the bloodhound, used to a tropical climate, confined his trips outside strictly to what needed to be taken care of, then it was back inside for an extended nap stretched out in front of the fire.

I nudged Josie and nodded my head at the two sets of front paws that were perched on the windowsill. Captain and Chloe were standing on their back legs and staring out the window at Jackson's plow that was making short work of the six inches of snow that had accumulated during the night.

"Hold your horses," I said, rubbing their heads. You know you can't go out there while Jackson is plowing. He'll be done soon."

Captain woofed at Jackson to hurry up then glanced up at me.

"I'm still worried about him down there in that heat," Josie said, kneeling down to hug the Newfie.

"I think he'll be fine," I said. "But that is quite the fur coat he's wearing."

"Our air conditioning bill is going to be enormous. You do know that, right?"

I shrugged it off as my phone buzzed, and I checked the number then answered.

"Hey, Mom. Yeah, it's still snowing," I said, then held the phone away from my ear until she stopped laughing. "Good for you." I looked over at Josie. "She's got a hot date and wants to know what she should wear."

"She's coming to us for fashion tips?" Josie said. "She must be desperate."

"Or drunk. Hang on, Mom. I'm gonna put you on speaker."

I set the phone down on the reception counter.

"Hi, Mrs. C.," Josie said. "Got a hot date, huh?"

"Hello, dear. Well, I wouldn't actually call it hot. At least, not yet."

"Good for you, Mom. What does he do?"

"He's the executive chef at one of the resorts down here."

The lightbulb went on immediately. I shook my head and glanced at Josie who still hadn't made the connection. Then she chuckled.

"And you thought you'd check him out and see if he might be interested in a new position, right?"

"Well, darling, we are going to need a chef for the restaurant. Chef Claire is only going to be around three or four months out of the year."

"That's true, Mom. Where's he taking you?"

"Oh, he's coming here. He's cooking for me."

"So, this is more of a job interview than a date?" I said, frowning.

"A little of both I guess," she said. "It'll probably depend on how much champagne we have."

"Then I'd go with that floral wraparound I got you for Christmas."

"Good thinking, darling. I'll do that," she said. "Oh, I almost forgot to mention that all the licenses and permits for both the restaurant and shelter are approved."

"Already?"

"Yes. You sound surprised."

"That was quick. Gerald, right?"

"Of course.

"Why is the Finance Minister worrying about some business permits and zoning issues?"

"He said he owed you a favor. And Gerald does a lot more than just move money around, darling."

"Yes, Mom. I'm very aware of that."

"Don't be too hard on him. He was just doing his job."

"If you say so," I said, staring out the window and waving at Jackson. "Any news on what's happening with Bill and Jerry?"

"I knew there was something else I needed to tell you. Actually, there is. Big news, in fact. Bill caught the right judge and was granted bail."

"Really? Two counts of murder and he was offered bail? That's a little loose even by Cayman standards, wouldn't you say?"

"Not necessarily. But I did hear that the judge is, all of a sudden, looking at some beach property not far from here."

"Let me guess. The judge just had a recent windfall," I said, shaking my head at Josie.

"I believe his story is that it was an inheritance," my mother said, laughing.

"And Bill and Jerry are lawyered up, and doing everything they can to string the process out for as long as they can, right?"

"No. Actually, they're gone," my mother said.

"What? No way."

"Yes, two nights ago, they simply vanished. And they also somehow managed to get all their money out."

"And gone to a place with no extradition treaty," I said.

"That's our guess, yes."

"Is anybody going to be looking for them?"

"Maybe a little," my mother said. "But probably not for long and not very hard."

"It's nice to have money, right?"

"Oh, don't say it like that, darling," she said, laughing. "Put a little zip in it. It's *nice* to have *money*!"

"I gotta go, Mom. Have fun on your dinner date. Love you."

"Love you, darling. You too, Josie. Enjoy the snowstorm."

"Have fun, Mrs. C."

I put my phone away and sat down. Chloe hopped up on my lap and rolled over on her back and waited for her tummy rub.

"Your mother is an unstoppable force. And you, my friend, are the immovable object."

"Former immovable object," I said. "From now on, when it comes to her, I'm just going to go with the flow."

"I'll believe it when I see it," she said, then looked at the front door. "Hey, Jackson. Thanks for taking care of the plowing."

"No problem," he said, stamping snow off his boots. "They're saying we might get another foot."

"Lovely," I said, trailing my fingernails up and down Chloe's stomach.

"Look at her," Josie said, laughing. "She's in a trance."

"Any chance I can get one of those?" Jackson said, grinning at me.

"Absolutely. Just as soon as you grow two more legs," I said.

"Sure. I'm lucky if I can get a quick hug out of you. But you'll take your top off for any old stingray that happens to swim by."

I glared at Josie.

"Really?"

She gave me a blank stare and shrugged her shoulders.

"What can I say? It's a story that needs to be told," she deadpanned, then grinned at Jackson. "And then retold as many times as possible."

A New Series from B.R. Snow!

The Whiskey Run Chronicles

The Whiskey Run Chronicles is the latest series from bestselling author B.R. Snow, and is set in the Thousand Islands during Prohibition when smuggling whiskey across the Canadian border into the U.S. was a business a lot of people wanted to get into. One of those people is Milo Razner, a man with big plans and a charming personality that belies a mean streak that sometimes seems to have a mind of its own. And soon after arriving in town, Milo begins to unveil his grand plan to become a respected, legitimate businessman while also operating the largest illegal booze running operation around.

The Whiskey Run Chronicles is written in individual episodes that are approximately 40-50 pages long and designed to be read in a single sitting. Readers can expect to see 3-4 new episodes every month, each one selling for less than a dollar, and the series will play itself out from just before Prohibition becomes the law of the land until it is finally repealed in the early 1930s.

The series has all the elements of B.R. Snow's writing style readers have come to expect and enjoy. The big cast of supporting characters are well-defined, and the dialogue pops off the page. It's a series that is one part historical fiction, one part crime story, and one part love story. Above all, it is smart and funny, and readers will find themselves rooting for Milo, a villain with a big heart and even bigger ideas about what might be possible when you do everything in your power to give the people what they want.

Episode 1 – *The Dry Season Approaches*

Milo Razner arrives in town and immediately begins to launch his plans to control the smuggling of illegal whiskey from Canada into the U.S. just before Prohibition becomes the law of the land. But before he can get started, he needs to make a couple of purchases and deal with a few locals he needs to help him get his grand plan off the ground.

Episode 2 – *Friends and Enemies*

Milo has a to-do list a mile long, and the increasingly lustful intentions of Ruby Crankovitch are making it difficult for him to concentrate. And when Oscar Hyde, the local chief of police, sets his sights on Milo, he is forced to add yet another item to his list of things to do. But Milo continues to march forward with his plan forward, and things are looking promising until Billy Crankovitch throws Milo a curve he isn't quite ready for.

Episode 3 – *Let the Games Begin*

Milo has been heeding his own advice and continuing to take the long-view. But he's increasingly anxious to get his new enterprise rolling. And when his new boat arrives, and the first batch of finished product is finally ready for delivery, Milo doesn't waste any time. But between having to deal with Ruby and a couple of problem employees, as well as the Senator's business partner who seems determined about getting to know Beulah a whole lot better, Milo has a lot of things to worry about. But when he learns that the new Prohibition agent assigned to crack down on the illegal booze business is an ex-cop he has a history with, things take a strange turn as Milo is confronted with his biggest challenge yet.

Episode 4 – *Enter the Revenuer*

Roland Doyle, the newly appointed local Prohibition agent, has arrived in town and is immediately determined to figure out of some way to make his mark and get promoted back to what he considers civilization. But Roland has a bit drinking problem and a newfound fear of water and boats that are making it difficult for him to achieve his goal. And since Milo has a history with Roland, he decides to lend a hand and do everything in his power to make sure the alcoholic, incompetent agent is both successful and stuck right where he is.

Episode 5 – *A Changing Landscape*

With Oscar Hyde, the local chief of police, in jail for bootlegging, and Roland Hyde's drinking out of control, Milo is hoping to be able to relax and enjoy himself a bit. But with a handful of unhappy employees, Ruby's demands that are rapidly getting out of control, and Billy finding a new love of his life, Milo finds himself dealing with problems on several fronts. And when he is forced to add a new business partner, Milo's world becomes even more complex as his business continues to grow.

Episode 6 – *Entrepreneurial Spirits*

Expansion is on Milo's mind as he makes some major decisions about the business as well as dabbling a bit in real estate. But threatening to put a major crimp in his plans are several of his employees who are either about ready to jump ship, or out to prove to Milo that they can run things better than he can. To make matters even worse is a local schoolteacher, the new love of Billy's life, who is hiding a secret that has definitely gotten Milo's attention and is pushing him to the edge of his already severely tested patience.

Episode 7 – *All Hands On Deck*

In the final episode of Volume 1, several problems Milo has been dealing with come into sharp focus as he attempts to take a bit of luster off of Roland Doyle's star that is beginning to shine brightly with some decision-makers in D.C. And with the assistance of Tom Collins and Birdie, along with help from an unexpected source, Milo sets forth with a plan do just the right amount of damage to Roland's reputation while continuing to focus the expansion of his burgeoning business that is struggling to keep pace with the seemingly endless thirst of his customers.

☆☆

Here's a sample of what some of the early readers are saying:

"I'm trying hard to fit The Whiskey Run Chronicles into a specific genre. It's certainly one part crime story, one part love story, and it definitely sits inside the boundaries of historical fiction. But there's something different about this series that I can't quite put my finger on that makes it hard to pigeonhole. It's smart, often very funny, but the series has a heart to it that I find incredibly appealing. And I don't think I've ever found myself rooting for a bad guy like I do Milo Razner. Rather than overthink it, my plan is to anxiously wait for each new episode to arrive, then sit down with a glass of bourbon and enjoy my journey back to the 1920s."

☆☆

"Two of my favorite aspects of Snow's writing, great characters driven by razor-sharp dialogue, are on full display, and the use of an episodic-structure, while different, works perfectly. This is going to be one hell of a great series!"

The Whiskey Run Chronicles

B.R. Snow

Episode 1

The Dry Season Approaches

Three Shots to the Wind

Milo nodded to the well-dressed man in black he passed on his way to the bar. He wasn't a huge fan of fedoras as a rule, but they had their time and place. Just like the one on Milo's head here and now. And Milo had to give the man credit for the way he wore his. Like he was confident about how good he looked; proud of the hat, and not apologizing at all for looking like a bit of a dandy.

Hats were tricky to pull off as far as Milo was concerned. A lot of folks pulled them down way too far, then made it worse by keeping their heads down when they walked past you. Like they were hiding something or weren't quite as confident as they were trying to appear. When that happened, Milo always got the impression that the hat was wearing the person, not the other way around.

Yeah, hats were tricky.

But if you got the angle of the hat cocked *just right*, held your head high, and looked people in the eye when you passed them on the street, you'd always get a nod out of Milo.

Even if you did look like a bit of a dandy.

Milo tipped his hat to a group of three women standing in the hotel lobby near the entrance to the bar. Working girls, he decided when he caught their taunting smiles and eyes that lingered just a touch too long.

"Ladies, I hope you're all doing well this beautiful evening," Milo said, continuing past them toward the bar.

"We could all be doing a lot better," one of the women said.

The other two women laughed, and the one who'd spoken to Milo met his eyes when he stopped and turned around. She cocked her head and stared at him, oozing confidence. No hat needed on this pretty young thing, Milo decided.

"I guess everyone could always be doing better, right?" Milo said.

"Indeed. I like your hat," the woman said, studying his fedora. "I never wear them myself."

"Because it would be redundant, right?"

"I beg your pardon?"

"Nothing. Merely a passing thought on my part. I'm Milo."

"Daisy," she said, glancing over her shoulder at her two companions before locking eyes with him again. "That's Maxine. This is Betsy."

"It's very nice to meet you ladies," Milo said, bowing slightly. "I hope you all have a wonderful evening."

"If you're looking for some company, feel free to stop by Fannie's later," Daisy said. "I'm sure I could make your stay here much more pleasant. Or, if your tastes run in that direction, all three of us."

Milo smiled and continued to match her stare.

"That's very thoughtful of you. Unfortunately, I have some business to attend to at the moment. But I must say, if I were ever honored to be in your company, Miss Daisy, including anyone else would be a pointless gesture. An exercise in futility if you will. For I would hate to ruin my reputation as a gentleman since I would undoubtedly be completely ignoring everyone else who happened to be present at the time."

Her two colleagues tittered and Daisy flushed bright red, but before she had a chance to recover and respond, Milo tipped his hat again, then turned and entered the bar. He glanced around and decided to sit at the bar. The bartender, a tall man who barely looked old enough to drink, approached and nodded his head at the three women who were still hovering near the entrance.

"Not many men can say no to Daisy," the bartender said, wiping down the mahogany in front of Milo.

"I didn't say no," Milo said. "I just said not now."

"Well, Daisy is a right now kind of girl and not used to men having to think about it," he said, laughing. "But judging by the way she's hanging in the doorway, I think you got her attention. What can I get you?"

"I think I'll have a beer with a back."

"Whiskey?"

"Actually, I heard a rumor that if I ask you real nice, you'll bring me a taste of some local refreshment."

"Who told you that?" the bartender said, now on alert.

"Just a guy who likes to spread rumors."

"I hate guys like that."

"Me too. But sometimes the rumormongers can be useful."

"Useful as in finding out where to get the best local shine?"

"Yes, among other things," Milo said, smiling. "Don't worry, your secret is safe with me."

"The hotel doesn't know I bring it in. It's only for special customers," the bartender said, wiping his hands with a fresh towel. "But when you're working for tips, you do what you can, right?"

"Yeah, I get that. By the way, I'm Milo Razner."

"Nice to meet you, Milo. My name's Tom. Tom Collins."

"Tom Collins. After the cocktail? That's a good name for a bartender I would imagine," Milo said, nodding.

"Actually, my name is Jerry Collins. But a buddy gave me the nickname when I was working in a joint that only sold moonshine. Most women can't stand the taste of it, so I started messing around with different juices and fruits you could use to make the shine go down easier. I got kind of a reputation for my concoctions."

"And the nickname stuck?"

"Yeah. And the name's a real conversation starter," Tom said.

"And good for tips, right?"

"You're a quick study, Milo."

"You have no idea, Tom Collins."

Tom reached below the bar and poured clear liquid into a shot glass.

"You want to join me?" Milo said. "I'm buying."

"Thanks, but I'm working," Tom said, shaking his head. "This stuff will set your brain on fire. Two of those and I wouldn't be able to make change."

"What is it?" Milo said, holding up the shot glass and staring at it up against the light.

"Billy calls it his Midnight Miracle," Tom said. "A hundred and fifty proof but smoother than Daisy's skin right after she gets out of the bath."

"Should I ask how you know that?" Milo said, still staring into the shot glass.

"It's no secret how Daisy makes her living," Tom said, shrugging. "I learned about her soft skin a long time ago. But that was back in the days when I could still afford her."

"I see," Milo said, holding the shot glass to his nose. "I'm getting the scent of something sweet."

"Billy won't tell me what that is," Tom said. "But I think he uses a touch of maple syrup."

"Interesting," Milo said. "Well, here goes nothing."

Milo tossed the shot back and felt the warmth surge through him, then it subsided and left him at a loss for words.

"Good, huh?" Tom said, nodding.

"Remarkable. Who's Billy?"

"Billy Crankovitch. He's a local. We go way back. And when it comes to making shine, I think he's a genius."

"And he makes moonshine for a living?"

"Nah. It's only a way for him to make a few extra bucks on the side. I do my best to help him out by selling some of it here."

"What does he do for a living?" Milo said, gesturing for another shot.

"Well, he's a dairy farmer. But as his wife keeps reminding him, he's just not a very good one."

"Ah, farmers. Salt of the earth. I'd like to meet this Mr. Crankovitch," Milo said, holding up the fresh shot to the light again. "It's crystal clear."

"I'm sure that can be arranged," Tom said. "He'll start cooking this year's batch as soon as he gets his corn harvested. But if he's got any of last year's batch left, you can buy a quart for three bucks."

"Twelve dollars a gallon?"

"What?"

"Nothing. Just doing some math in my head."

Milo and Tom both looked toward the lobby when they heard the swelling noise that was punctuated with shouts and protests.

"Somebody's not happy," Milo said, glancing around at the crowd.

"Beulah must be here," Tom said. "She's speaking tonight in the ballroom."

Milo looked at Tom and waited for more.

"Beulah Peppin. She's the head of the local temperance movement."

"Ah, yes," Milo said. "The Women's Christian Temperance Union. The WCTU seems to be everywhere these days. Which one is Mrs. Peppin?"

"Miss Peppin," Tom said. "And she's the one in the white dress."

Milo studied the young woman who continued to casually give instructions to several people who were surrounding her even as the shouts of protests continued to swell.

"I take it she has her detractors," Milo said.

"Yeah, and I'm one of them. What is it with some people? They're always on a mission to ruin everybody else's fun. The way the winters are around here, if you take away people's right to drink, they'll be nothing to do six months out of the year."

"Yes, I'm afraid the Dries have gotten a lot of traction," Milo said, downing the second shot and again having the same reaction. "This is truly a remarkable concoction."

"Lucky for us, the President vetoed that stupid law, huh?" Tom said.

"Congress is getting ready to override his veto," Milo said, taking a sip of beer.

"But they won't be able to pass it, right?"

"Oh, I'm certain the veto is going to be overridden."

"How do you know that?"

"I've been told that by some people I know in Washington," Milo said.

"You have friends in Washington?"

"Oh, my, no," Milo said, laughing. "I would never call the people I know in Washington friends. They're just lawyers who managed to convince enough voters they're worthy of making decisions on their behalf."

"I take it you're not much of a fan of politicians," Tom said.

"I dislike politicians," Milo said. "But I detest lawyers. Combine the two, and you get a very nasty product."

"Like bad moonshine," Tom said.

"Yes. If it doesn't kill you, the odds are it will leave you blind," Milo said, gesturing for a third shot.

"You want another?"

"One more."

"Be careful. This stuff sneaks up on you in a hurry."

"Let's call the third one additional field study. Sort of a personal research project."

"It's your funeral," Tom said, pouring the shot. "By the way, what are you doing in town?"

"Actually, I have just relocated to your wonderful town. This is my first day here."

"Really? What do you do for work?"

"I'm currently in transition, and I'm looking for a change. Something in my head is telling me that it's time to do something different."

"Like what?"

"I thought I might give dairy farming a shot," Milo said, tossing back his third shot. "Whew. I see what you mean about it sneaking up on you."

"Uh, no offense, Milo," Tom said. "You could have given me a hundred guesses, and I wouldn't have come up with dairy farmer. You know much about cows?"

"Other than they have four legs and produce milk, not a single thing."

"Okay. I guess you gotta start somewhere, right? Look, Milo, dairy farming is no picnic. And there aren't any days off. You do know that cows have to be milked twice a day every day, don't you?"

"I did not know that," Milo said, shaking his head. "I'm glad I stopped by, Tom Collins. Not only have you provided me with some of the best alcohol I have ever tasted, but you've also taught me something."

"Why on earth would you want to be a dairy farmer?"

"Well, there's just something calling me to it. When booze is outlawed, I have a gut feeling that my milk is going to be in very high demand. And I always try to go with my gut instincts."

Milo shook his head to clear it and glanced back at Beulah Peppin who was still chatting with several people milling around her.

"She is a very striking woman," Milo said.

"She is. Too bad she never seems to put her looks on better display. It's like she does everything she can to hide them," Tom said. "But I do like her hat."

"Yes, I agree. And she wears it very well."

Made in the USA
Columbia, SC
16 June 2017